The Independent Bookworm

About the Book

To live as a normal human, Lydia has to catch up on several years of school in several subjects. However, the dragon's Council insists she become their queen—without Colin. For the sake of peace, Lydia agrees to visit the dragons' realm, to reconnect with their way of life. At the same time she hires a tutor because giving up her dreams is not an option.

Colin worries whether he's ready for the love of a dragoness. Can he, as a human, do justice to a relationship this early in his life? Or is he doomed to hurt Lydia one day?

Although Harm takes care of his biological father, he avoids talking to him. How is he supposed to handle all the lies he had been told over the years? And then there's Nicole who slowly but inevitably captures his heart although she still fights the idea that dragons or magic exist.

And Mordekay too hasn't given up. He simply adjusted his plans to the new situation. Now humanity's freedom and the survival of a whole species are under threat. Can the friends defeat him permanently without forcing Lydia to accept the crown?

About the Author

Ever since she was born, Katharina Gerlach had her head in the clouds. She and her three younger brothers grew up in the middle of a forest in the heart of the Luneburgian Heather. After romping through the forest with imagination as her guide, the tomboy learned to read and disappeared into magical adventures, past times or eerie fairytale woods.

She never returned to Earth for long, although she managed to successfully finish training as a landscape gardener, study forestry and gain a PhD. But then, she discovered her vocation: storytelling and realized she'd have to write to make her dream of sharing her stories with others come true.

Katharina loves to write Fantasy, Science Fiction and Historical Novels for all age groups. At present, she is writing at her next project in a small house near Hildesheim, Germany, where she lives with her husband, three children and a dog.

more information: www.KatharinaGerlach.com

Tried by Fire

Katharina Gerlach
and Leonie Joy

Tried by Fire
published by the Independent Bookworm, USA und D
This book is also available as eBook. It has been published in English and in German.

If you find any typos or formatting problems in this eBook, please contact the publisher (www.IndependentBookworm.de).

editor: Ethan James Clarke
printed On-Demand Publishing LLC, 100 Enterprise Way, Suite A200, Scotts Valley, CA 95066, USA, www.createspace.com

ISBN-13 978-3-95681-110-4

More information can be found on the publisher's website:
http://www.IndependentBookworm.de

For my family. I couldn't have done it without you.

TABLE OF CONTENTS

HIGH SCHOOL DRAGONS 1: KISSED BY FIRE
Fantasy Romance

It is highly recommended to read volume one of the trilogy first.

The flames of a car crash have killed Lydia's parents and erased her former life from her mind. To be able to go on, she seals her emotions in a hidden corner of her mind. She no longer cares that she's got to live with a foster mother or that she must to go to school again. The world has lost all color, all scent, and all sense.

But on her first day in Hilldale High School, she meets two young men that break through her barriers. Harm—strong, dark, and strangely old-fashioned—lights up her senses. And then, there's Colin, whose gentle jokes and easy camaraderie soothe her soul and fill her with peace.

When a waste paper basket spontaneously ignites on its own, Lydia begins to dream of dragons. Will she be able to find out who she is and what she wants before her past catches up with her?

available as eBook and in print
ISBN-13 978-3-95681-091-6

PROLOG

Nicole stared at herself in the mirror on the wardrobe in her cluttered room and worried her lower lip like she'd done every so often during the last three months. She pondered the same problem every time.

Dragons. That's not possible. I must have dreamed.

Her gaze wandered from her freckles to the piles of books occupying every surface of her room. Had she read too many fantasy stories? Was her imagination running wild?

Mom always said that one day she'd find it hard to separate reality from dreams, and that she should read some 'real' books. But so far, Nicole hadn't been interested in the ones she'd recommended. What if her mother was right and that day had finally arrived?

But Colin had assured her that dragons existed. Maybe the two of them had accidentally eaten something that made them hallucinate. Or maybe her obsession with reading and making up stories had rubbed off on him. Because for sure something like dragons didn't exist. They were just as unreal as fairies or unicorns. If the girls in her school heard her claim that dragons existed, she'd be the target of every bad joke they could think of. So far, she'd always been happy that the in-girls hadn't noticed her. She had also been proud that she wasn't like the other girls in school.

"It's time to grow up." She looked at her mirror-self again, lifting her chin. "I'll be like everyone else and the hallucinations or whatever else they are will vanish."

With new determination she fetched a couple of cardboard boxes and began to pack all her books, although she felt as if someone was ripping her heart out. Maybe the local library would take them. Or the used book shop. They needn't know about her pain or her craziness.

FIRST CHAPTER

"I'm not a nurse, you know." As Mordekay pressed his newly acquired mobile to his ear, he kept his voice low so it wouldn't wake his barn-sized patient. "He's been mostly sleeping. For months on end. Guess who's the one forced to take care of him. If it weren't my own body I'm helping, I'd have put Dragon Bane into him a long time ago."

He listened to the words on the other side without sparing a glance at the white washed walls, the shuttered windows, or the neon overhead light of the warehouse they were staying in.

"Don't you know that Harm keeps ordering me with the Commanding Voice? How am I to get away from that?" The face he was currently wearing—hated because it wasn't his own—showed Blackfeather's smooth Native American features. However, they contorted into a mask of barely suppressed rage. "My own son is ordering me around like a slave." His fingers clenched around the mobile until it groaned from the strain. "What?" He forced himself to relax his hand. "Yes, I know that he isn't really my son. But still … I had high plans for him, and instead he goes and fraternizes with … *humans*." He spat out

13

the last word as if it were dirt he'd accidentally eaten. Then he listened to the voice on the other end of the line.

"You are right. I completely forgot about catnip since I've never tried it. Are you sure it'll work?" A smile grew on his face. "Perfect. A little vomiting won't kill him, and if it helps me, I'm game to try."

With his mobile still on his ear, he turned on his swivel chair and looked at the black mass snoring gently on a thin layer of gold. It was an impressive sight, and a sliver of longing tugged at what he considered his heart. If only he could drive that traitor from his body and slip back into it where he belonged. He sighed. "I just wish there was an easy way to swap bodies. But of course the kids won't be stupid enough to fall for the same ritual twice."

He listened once more. "Wait a minute. Are you trying to tell me that there's another way to get it back?" His features relaxed the longer his dialog partner talked. When the explanation was over, Mordekay grinned. "How hard can it be to find a witch?"

The black dragon in the hall moaned and blinked into the bright light. It was obviously waking up.

"I gotta go for now, but I'll call you back about that," Mordekay said. "You can already get started on locating a witch."

As Harm lifted his hand to the door of the warehouse's side entrance, his heart felt like a stone. Why did it have to rub in his chest so? He wiped his eyes and forced the frown from his face. It was hard enough facing a new father who surely had new expectations. He didn't need a sermon about gratitude or an artificial father-son talk. He needed Blackfeather to wake up and return to school. Harm loathed himself for forcing the dean to believe that Mr. Smolinsky was ill for so long, but at least his father still had the job. With a sigh, he straightened his shoulders and opened the door.

Inside, everything was like before. Mordekay in Blackfeather's body sulked while shoveling dragon poo into a wheelbarrow—great manure, if one believed Angie—and the black dragon lay as still as ever. But when he rounded the giant body, he noticed that his father had moved after all. The head, usually curled up with the snout under his right wing, was now resting close to the table and chair Mordekay used during his breaks, and his breathing had become deeper.

With his heart hammering in his chest, Harm stepped closer and touched the smooth, black scales on the dragon's cheek. Behind him, the warehouse door creaked as Mordekay wheeled his load to the dung heap behind the warehouse.

"Father?" The word felt like a stone in Harm's mouth. He'd never addressed Mordekay that way, and although he knew that the black dragon no longer was Mordekay, his heart contracted whenever he used the word. He breathed deeply and spoke again. "Wakey, wakey, Father."

His voice echoed in the big warehouse. Before it had completely died away, Blackfeather opened his eyes. For a while he stared at the wall, eyes unfocused and only half open, but soon he blinked and sat up.

"Where am I?" His voice boomed through the hall as if amplified. He winced and whispered his next question. "What am I?"

"You're in Mordekay's body." Harm told him what had happened in as few words as possible, ending with, "You've been out cold for three months."

Blackfeather examined his oversized new body "How did you get me here?"

"We flew. It seems that the body instinctively knows how that works." Harm pretended to sort some papers on Mordekay's table. He didn't look at his father. It made talking easier. "When we arrived here, the wound in your side opened again, probably from the strain, and you fell unconscious. Luckily you were inside the warehouse already, so no one saw you."

"What about Mordekay?" Blackfeather sat up and his head swung around, his gaze searching the room.

"I ordered him to take care of you." Harm grinned. "Believe me, he doesn't like it. I'm using the Commanding Voice. He's got no choice but to obey."

Blackfeather chuckled, a deep rumbling that emanated from his chest. It was a sound Harm had never heard from the black dragon before. Strangely enough, it triggered a memory of Nicole in the clearing on that fateful day as she stared at the black dragon, unable to fully focus because of the drugs in her blood.

"I think it's time to take him back home. The Council will surely hold a trial," Blackfeather said when he finished laughing.

"That's not possible as long as we don't have a new queen." Harm turned and forced himself to look at the big, black dragon. Instinctively, his hands balled into fists. He had to recall that it was not Mordekay staring at him from yellow, slitted eyes. "We have to stay here and convince Lydia that she has to take the job regardless of her feelings for Colin. And for that, you'll have to turn into Mordekay's human form."

"I don't want to be Mr. Smolinsky." Blackfeather shook his head. "He's ugly and mean."

"But he's teaching sciences to Lydia. He's important." The chair Harm fetched to sit on scraped over the concrete floor with a screeching sound that nearly drowned out Mordekay's return despite the wheelbarrow's noise.

"How do I turn into a human?" Blackfeather lifted his wings in a gesture of confusion. "Shouldn't it happen instinctively?"

"It's not difficult." Harm shrugged. "You picture your human self in your mind and fill it with your inner magic."

The dragon closed his eyes and breathed deeply. Nothing happened.

Harm waited some more, but there was still no change.

Mordekay snorted. "Did you think accessing a dragon's magic would be easy for a human?"

"Changing form goes with the body. It requires no external energy since it's inborn." Harm turned to Mordekay and twisted his voice into command mode. "Go to sleep for now."

The traitor crumbled. Harm caught him before he slammed into the ground and carried him to his bed where he laid him down. It was better to have the traitor out of the way for now. He turned back to Blackfeather. "The magic should be within your body. Can't you feel it, at least a little?"

"I think I found it. It's a bit like electricity, right?" Blackfeather's voice sounded strained.

KAZING

A flash took out the electricity in the room, and Blackfeather collapsed. Harm was just about fast enough to evade the big, crashing head. He groaned. Couldn't his father get the easiest spell right? Now he had to wait again for him to regain consciousness. If only he had someone he could ask.

An idea occurred to him. He needed to talk to White Crow. Lydia's old mentor seemed to know a lot about dragons. Maybe he could help.

"Wake up," he ordered Mordekay. "Make sure no one disturbs my father in your body, and get the electricity going again."

"Yes, master." Mordekay's voice held an edge of anger but he bowed and went to fetch some tools.

When Harm arrived at Lydia's parents' house, it seemed deserted, but as soon as he entered, White Crow was behind him.

"The traitor's son." He cocked his head and crossed his arms in front of his chest.

Harm's stomach fell. The Native American didn't look as if he was willing to help him.

"I'm not Mordekay's son." Harm explained his relationship to Blackfeather, and his father's love for Mordekay's wife. "So in truth, I'm Blackfeather's son. It's he that needs your help."

"The humans' way of talking seems to rub off on you," White Crow said and pointed to the door to the living room. "Take a seat and tell me what Blackfeather needs."

Harm didn't need to be told twice. Although it was strange sitting in the dark room with the furniture barely visible, it felt great to unburden himself. He told White Crow all about the encounter with Mordekay and how Blackfeather had taken over the dragon's body. "And now he can't tap into his new body's magic to turn into a human." He expected White Crow to laugh at this minor problem, but the man shook his head and scratched his beard as if the situation was life-threatening. His eyebrows rose and he bent forward to better see the man. "Is it that bad?"

"If he can't access the magic, he'll explode, taking everyone with him who's close enough." White Crow pulled a pipe from his pocket and stuffed it. "Do you know why dragons can turn into humans? I could tell you while I think about a solution for your father."

Since Harm was sure it wouldn't be a good idea to hurry White Crow, he he leaned back and forced himself to be patient. The man was too focused in everything he did. Trying to rush him would only lead to disaster.

He had to wait until White Crow emptied his pipe and said, "And now, let's go to your father and see what I can do. I do believe I know a way to help him."

White Crow crouched beside Blackfeather's massive body and shook his head. "It shouldn't be this difficult. Did Mordekay do something aside from the ritual before he was forced out of his body?"

"Not that I know of," Blackfeather said.

"Try again. It's really important."

The dragon closed his eyes in concentration. Harm closed his eyes too, feeling for his father's magic like White Crow had explained. He was still surprised by how much the Native American knew about dragons and their magic.

There ... the electrical zing reverberated through his veins. That must be the magic Blackfeather couldn't access. For a moment he hesitated. What if he let his father figure it out on his own? He shrugged. It wasn't as if he could wait. If Blackfeather didn't learn how to turn into a human, they'd have to leave, which meant leaving behind all of his new friends; the first friends he'd ever had. Also, there was the threat of a magic explosion which would endanger a lot of people. Harm mentally tugged at the magic again, ignoring the tingle that spread through his mind. Gently he guided the magic toward Blackfeather's consciousness. When he noticed his father groping around blindly, he shoved the thread of magic his way. It connected.

Boom—

Pain lanced through Harm's mind and he reeled back from the impact. Blinking, he fought dizziness, nausea, and a blackness that threatened to swallow him. Only a stray thought of Nicole kept him from passing out.

"Harm!" The voice was familiar, but not its tone. It sounded deeply worried. "I didn't mean to hurt you." Arms closed around him.

Angrily, Harm shook them off. "Don't touch me." He struggled to stand, surprised that he'd been sitting on the ground in the first place. He must have fallen when the magic backfired. He blinked some more and focused on the small man standing in front of him. "At least we've got you in human shape."

His father turned and picked up a small mirror from the table. His face fell. "I look like Smolinsky."

"As expected," White Crow said. "After all, Mordekay has your body now. What surprised me was the clash of your and Harm's magic."

Harm's stomach was still in turmoil, so he sat on the table's wobbly chair. Somehow it felt good to know that White Crow didn't know everything after all. Satisfied that he wouldn't have to leave and that Blackfeather wouldn't blow up, he closed his eyes and allowed his exhaustion to claim its due.

Second Chapter

*N*icole carried her heavy backpack downstairs, drawn by the smell of cheese melting on toast. Gosh, she was hungry. She put the backpack down beside the door with a thud. Its dark leather contrasted nicely with the cream wallpaper. Still half asleep, she sat down at the kitchen table.

"What's in there? Bricks?" Her brother grinned and stuffed some more toast into his mouth.

"Books. From the library." Nicole grabbed some toast.

"But you only took them out a few days ago." Colin's eyebrows rose. "You can't have finished reading them already."

"None of your business." A pang went through Nicole's heart. She really, really had wanted to read those books. But look where it got her.

"Lydia asked if we'd like to go for an ice cream this afternoon." Colin checked the money in his purse. He was probably trying to gauge whether it'd be enough for lunch at school and an ice cream. Nicole smiled a little at his inability to keep his money together. He looked up. "Are you coming, or what?"

Nicole shook her head, though it seemed as heavy as a millstone. She liked Lydia, but right now she just couldn't face her.

"Oh, come on. Harm will be there too. It'll be fun to hang out with the dragons."

"There. Are. No. Dragons." Nicole ground her teeth just as their mother entered with a couple of fresh kitchen towels.

"Stop it, Nicole," she said as she put them away.

Colin bent forward and stared at his sister, concern written all over his face. "We're only going to have an ice cream after school. You'll like it."

"What a nice idea," their mother chimed in and put two more slices of toast on the table. "It'd give me some free time this afternoon where I can finally sort out your birthday presents."

"I'll hate you all talking about dragons." Nicole pressed her lips together, fighting down a wave of fear. Ridiculous! Harm and Lydia were her friends regardless of whether they were crazy or not. Still, she wasn't ready to face them yet.

"Dragons?" Their mother glared at Nicole. "Are you trying to put flees in your brother's ears again? There's no such thing as a dragon. Get a grip on reality."

"That's what I'm trying." Nicole glared back. She'd had this argument with her mother once too often. "This time it's Colin who insists that dragons exist."

"Colin?" Their mother turned and lifted an eyebrow.

"That's a game, silly." Colin got up, not looking at his mother, grabbed his lunch packet and his backpack and walked toward the door. "Well, I'll be at the ice cream parlor in the mall with Lydia and Harm after school. You're very welcome to join us there, Nicole."

"I think that's a very good idea. Lydia is such a nice young girl, the perfect friend."

Her mother kept talking but Nicole neither answered nor listened. She knew very well that Lydia had become the best friend she'd ever had in the short time they'd known each other. But whatever nightmare she'd lived through had destroyed that. She'd seen Lydia as a white dragon, for crying out loud. And what was worse was that Lydia insisted that all of her muddled memories were true—as did her brother and Harm. They must have drugged her somehow. You didn't get hallucinations from nothing. And as long as she didn't know what really happened, she couldn't socialize with them. She wouldn't risk another drug-induced nightmare. It was time to find some new friends. Silently she grabbed her own lunch packet, hoisted the heavy backpack over her shoulder, placed a quick kiss on her mother's cheek, and left the house.

Nicole eyed the in-girls of her form chatting amiably as they passed the security checkpoint. Without her books, she felt very lonely. How did one make friends if one couldn't talk about books anymore? At least not about the ones she'd read before. Who would make a suitable friend? There weren't many girls that Isabella and her buddies didn't order around, and Nicole didn't fancy becoming one of them. But would she want to be another one of Isabella's buddies? Were Chelsea and Patricia happy to be friends with Isabella? The three had lost a lot of support when Lydia had faced them down, but they still strode through the corridors as if the school belonged to them. And the masses parted. Since their lockers were close to hers, she followed them.

"Guess what? My future sister-in-law went crazy." Isabella uttered a clearly artificial laugh. Nicole's heart missed a beat when she realized that Isabella still intended to become Colin's girlfriend. She inched closer. Isabella didn't seem to notice. "She's been giving away all her books. Those must have cost a fortune."

How did Isabella know? Nicole's finger grew cold.

"Bah," Chelsea said. "Who's interested in books?"

"And fantasy at that. I'd rather have this." Patricia pulled something from her pocket and showed it to the other girls. They ooh-ed and ah-ed, and she whispered, "It's supposed to make an orgasm even better."

Blushing, Nicole turned to her locker and tried not to listen any more, but Isabella turned to her.

"I bet your friend will need this pretty soon." She pressed a packet of condoms into Nicole's hand. Nicole dropped it like a hot coal, and the three girls laughed. Back before the 'incident', Nicole would have shot them down with a few choice words, but now … her heart fell. She wasn't prepared for a situation like this. With her lips pressed tightly together, she turned, grabbed her books from her locker, locked it, and hurried away with the girls' laughter still in her back. She didn't even look whether Patricia picked up her condoms again. However, the laughter didn't die down, so obviously the girls were following her. If only she could think of something to say that would make them like her.

"Redhead," Isabella called, but Nicole didn't stop. "Try not to set all the boys on fire." Chelsea and Patricia burst out laughing, but Nicole thought the joke rather flat. Fine. Teasing she could bear, and the classroom wasn't far.

Her foot was kicked sideways. She stumbled. Stretching out her hands, she tried to break her fall. Her books tumbled to the ground. Before she could follow them, two strong arms caught her. She looked up. When she realized it was Harm, she pushed him away hurriedly. "I don't need your help."

Harm's face clouded over. "I'm sorry if I offended you somehow."

Nicole's heart contracted. She hadn't meant to hurt his feelings. On the other hand, she wasn't ready for the complications his presence brought.

"Here, you dropped these." Chelsea handed her her books, looking only at Harm. She batted her eyelashes and addressed him. "You're a savior, you know."

Isabella chimed in, putting her arm around Nicole's shoulders. "Our Nicole's such a clumsy klutz sometimes. But I'm sure you know that already." Her smile was as false as it could be, even Nicole realized that, but it still felt good to have some friendly support, even if it was fake.

Patricia grabbed Harm's arm and clung to it. "We'd love to have a protector like you. I know you're in Smolinsky's class too. Why don't you accompany us?"

"I'm sorry for this misconception." Harm freed his arm with a little more strength than necessary and Patricia winced. "I am here for my friend." He took Nicole's books and her arm and led her toward the classroom. She could feel the gazes of the three girls burn into her back. A small smile tugged at her lips. Maybe it wasn't as hard as she'd thought to reconnect with Harm and Lydia.

"Did you know that Smolinsky will be back today?" Harm smiled down at her and her pulse quickened. Why had she never noticed before how handsome he was?

It took her a moment to find her voice. "I'm glad about that. He's much better at explaining things than his substitute."

"Well…" Harm hesitated. "I'm not sure how he'll hold up right now. After all, Blackfeather isn't as learned as Mordekay was."

"Mordekay? Blackfeather?" Wide-eyed, Nicole stared at Harm, stopping right in the middle of the hall. Did this nightmare never end?

"It's not easy for Blackfeather." Harm didn't seem to notice her discomfort. "He just learned how to turn his dragon body into his human form. I'm not optimistic whether he'll be up to teaching physics."

Nicole's mind whirled. He was talking about dragons just as casually as Colin. Was she only surrounded by crazies? It was physically impossible to turn a human into anything but a human—even with the best makeup artist in the world at hand it wouldn't be feasible. They had to be crazy. Or were they trying to drive her nuts? But why?

"Ehm." She reached for her books and decided it'd be better to be safe than sorry. "Thank you for your help, Harm, but I think I can make it from here." She fled into the classroom, trying to forget Harm's confused and hurt expression.

It had been more than three months since Nicole stopped talking to us altogether. I watched her sidle through the school's corridors, always alone. Gone was her cheerfully bossy attitude. She hadn't taken out a book from the library ever since we defeated Mordekay. Colin's worry about her was slowly getting to me. Why was it so hard for her to embrace the fact that dragons existed? I mean, she'd been the one reading all those fantasy stories and fairy tales. You'd think she would embrace her new knowledge.

"Angie said that she hasn't had enough time to digest the shock," Colin said as we licked our ice cream. Meeting in the mall had become our everyday afternoon ritual. My gaze lingered on Colin and I enjoyed the warmth his sight sent through my body like a wave. His voice was so melodious. "Also, the drugs and the spell Mordekay used on her distorted her perception, which might have triggered a lot of anxieties."

"That's all as it may be," Harm said, "but what can we do to help her?" He was on his third portion already.

Silence. As often as one of us posed this question, no one ever answered it. Was there no solution but giving her more time?

After some time, Harm spoke without looking at us. "We've got another problem." His gaze traveled over the old-fashioned, pastel-colored furniture, the bar and the mirror behind it. "Blackfeather refuses to shift. He has decided to remain in his human form for good, and White Crow thinks that that'll cost him his sanity in the long run. Magic grows in us permanently. You can't pile it up without consequences, but the idiot just doesn't want to see that."

"You're calling your own father an idiot?" I was taken aback. I never, ever would have called my parents names like that. The warmth of their love flooded through me at the thought.

"Well, I'm sorry, but he does behave like one." Harm pulled his eyebrows together, his anger barely suppressed. "Just because he saved your life doesn't mean I've gotten used to him being my father. With White Crow back in the dragon village, I've got to teach my father everything about dragons. It's like he's the little child and I'm the grown-up. I'm not happy about the situation right now."

Silence again. This was another topic I wasn't able to help with. How did you comfort someone whose whole life blew up overnight? Come to think of it, that was what had happened to Nicole too, but Harm seemed to cope better. For times on end, he got along just fine with Blackfeather. Only when there was some minor disagreement did he come close to bursting with anger. Colin once tried to say something but that backfired—literally. I had to use a magical shield to keep my love from going up in flames. I smiled at the memory of the kiss I got as a reward, when an idea occurred to me.

"Maybe we should talk to Angie again. She knows so much. I'm sure she can help with Blackfeather," I suggested. My foster mother was the best dragon I could think of, and the only one who just might be able to change Blackfeather's mind, given time. After all, she'd been living in human guise for a very long time already.

A little while later we were sitting around Angie's kitchen table sipping hot cocoa. The taste melted in my mouth with a warm sweetness that made me want to purr; a pity I wasn't a cat.

Colin explained Blackfeather's situation. "So we're worried that he'll get hurt if he doesn't use his inherent magic."

"I can talk to Blackfeather," Angie said, leaning back in her worn wooden chair. "I'm not sure how much it'll help, but I can try."

"What are *you* doing to keep your magic from ripping you apart?" Harm stared at her as if she were his salvation or damnation.

"Oh, I go for flights on clouded nights." Angie smiled, cocoa in the corner of her mouth. "I'll try to get Blackfeather to join me. I'm sure he'll love flying."

"Well, as long as that stops him from blowing apart." Harm shrugged.

"Who'd told you that?" Angie's eyebrows went up. "For most dragons, not using their magic results in cramps and a severe dizziness, not instantaneous self-combustion."

Colin set down his empty mug. "White Crow found an old report about a human in a dragon's body who blew up because he didn't or couldn't use his magic."

"White Crow?" Cocoa spilling everywhere, Angie was halfway over the table before any of us could react. "White Crow is dead!"

"Well, yes." I spoke before anyone else could say something. After all, White Crow had insisted we keep his survival a secret until he found the traitor. Not that I thought Angie a traitor, but I'd sworn to myself I'd protect White Crow's secret. "He put it in a book I fetched from the library at home, and I discovered it. He'd scribbled into the margins like a scholar."

"He so liked to read." Angie sat back down, ignoring the mess she'd made. "I miss him so much." Tears twinkled in her eyes, rolled over her cheek and landed on the table with a hard-edged clatter. I stared at the crystals, unbelieving. Angie was White Crow's wife? Oh, drat. My heart contracted so badly, I set aside my still half-full mug. How could I keep her from the love of her life? Ever since I met Colin, I've known what she must have gone through when she lost her mate. But I'd never, ever expected her partner to be a human. How come she'd never talked about him when I needed her advice so badly? Her experience with being married to a human could be what I needed to convince the Council that I needed Colin more than anyone else.

I stared at the others, who were discussing whether it was better to get Blackfeather to visit Angie or the other way around.

After a while, I pushed my whirling thoughts aside and joined the discussion. That evening, my friends left with a little more hope than the last few days. Maybe tomorrow I could get Nicole to come and talk to Angie too.

THIRD CHAPTER

*O*blivious of the classroom, Colin dreamed of Lydia and his heart filled with love. She had this inner glow that made her so beautiful to him. It wasn't her looks that touched his soul, it was her vibrancy. Just sitting beside her made him feel at home. The warmth of his love coursed through his veins, but a nagging thought remained. What if she fell in love with a dragon after all? Wouldn't it be better for both of them? But then he remembered Angie's words.

Dragons loved once, and once only. He smiled at the thought of growing old with Lydia. He could picture them with rounded bellies, wrinkles, and canes in a little condo in Florida, visited by their kids and grandchildren once in a while. He smiled until a thought crossed his mind.

What if Lydia accepted to become queen after all? Sure, she was dead set against it right now, but once she realized that being human was no bed of roses, she might change her mind. Would he be able to live with the dragons? Wouldn't they tease him or even bully him? What would he do then? His heart accelerated.

"… Colin?"

The sharp pain of an elbow stab from his desk mate ripped him from his thoughts. He stared at the expectant face of their history teacher, rubbing his ribs. It was obvious that the man had asked him a question. Colin gave the only answer he could possibly give. "I'm sorry, but I don't know."

The teacher shook his head and turned to someone else, and Colin pressed his lips together. Normally he knew the answers to the teacher's questions since he liked learning, so why did he find it so hard to concentrate on the lesson at hand? In his mind, Lydia's face pushed aside the classroom, but this time, he was aware of what was happening. With all of his willpower, he pushed thoughts of her aside and concentrated on what the teacher was telling them.

"Now you know that witch-hunts were not a phenomenon of the Middle Ages in general, and that even the Spanish Inquisition did not actively pursue witches," the teacher said. "The devastating hunting down of women and men considered witches began in the middle of the 15th century and claimed an estimated two hundred thousand lives. Even today, there are some countries in the world where witches are hunted and killed."

The rest of the lesson, Colin concentrated on the time when women weren't safe anywhere in the world; a time when anyone could point a finger on someone else to get them burnt at the stake; a time where more knowledge was lost to humans than they'd ever know. No wonder there weren't any true witches around. Together with thousands of innocent women and men, they'd been hunted down and murdered.

"The last known official witch trial took place in Poland in 1783, although two unnamed women were executed in Poznań, Poland, in 1793 as witches too. But their trials weren't legitimate. Not that it mattered much for the women." The bell rang just then and the teacher called over the ensuing hubbub, "Find out the names of the last witch-trial women in at least three cases and note them down with the year of their verdict and whether the sentence was carried out or not."

Colin made a short note in his mobile, stuffed it into his bag and hurried out of the room, squeezing past his classmates. He so longed to see Lydia again, his heart already contracted at the thought that the break was only a short one.

He found her in the main hall where she was watching Nicole, who sat on a radiator, staring out of a window, while Harm was standing close to her, frowning at three girls in ultra-modern clothing.

"She's so unhappy," Lydia said without turning to him. Had she felt his presence? Or was it his body odor? What if she didn't like the scent of the shower gel he'd used this morning?

Lydia turned, put her arms around him and dug her face into his chest, sending a wave of warm feelings through him. "I wish I knew what to do to help her. Angie says we'll have to give her time to adjust, but she's not making any progress at all. And she shuns me, and Harm. Can't you talk to her?"

Colin hated to disappoint her. "I've tried, but she gets all bristly and angry when I say something. Even if it's something not related to dragons. She even told me she's not interested in friends anymore, but at the same time she's doing her best to be accepted by Isabella and her buddies."

Lydia turned her head without letting go of him, jerking her nose at the three girls. "Are you talking about them?"

He nodded.

"What does she want with empty heads like them?" The despair in her voice pained him deeply.

"I don't know, but I trust Angie's advice." Maybe reminding Lydia that Angie had been right plenty of times would help. It did. Lydia relaxed a little and tore her gaze off her friend.

"Let's walk around for a while," she said.

When she remained silent for most of the break, Colin asked, "Are you getting along? You do know that you can ask me for help any time, don't you? I'm still officially your guide."

"The people are nice enough." Lydia sighed. "But I just can't wrap my head around most of the subjects. I'm okay with science, Spanish, and English. It's pretty much the same as what I learned back home. But history is all different. And don't get me started on social studies or music or art. There are so many things I don't know I feel like I'm a complete failure."

"Absolutely not!" Colin pulled her into his arms and looked into her wonderful, light blue eyes. "You've grown up in a completely different culture with completely different school subjects. You'll need a little time and some help to catch up with our stuff. That's all." He bent forward until his lips touched hers. Their warmth melted his core and he didn't know whether *he* was holding *her* up or the other way around. When first bell rang, he let go of her very reluctantly, drinking in her upturned face as if it was ambrosia for the soul. An idea occurred to him. "We could ask Angie if there's a way you can afford a tutor. I'm sure there are students who'd be able to help you."

"That is a great idea."

Colin blushed at the admiration in her gaze. To hide his embarrassment, he turned, took her arm and escorted her to her locker. "If you want me to, I can come with you after school."

"I'd love that," she said. "But don't forget our ice-cream hangout."

Her laughter still rang in his ears when he settled into his place in his science class.

I enjoyed two wonderful hours in the ice cream parlor with my friends—sans Nicole. Two hours where I didn't have to think about economic consequences of some tea that got thrown into a harbor or about the number and names of human presidents or some such. There was still plenty of time to learn all about them … after I got home.

Later, Colin and I entered Angie's cozy kitchen. Aside from my own room, it was the place I liked best in the whole house. My foster mother was preparing dinner, something with white beans and ground meat that smelled delicious.

"I'm nearly done," Angie said without turning. "And it should be enough for all of us, including Colin. Please lay the table."

I had to smile at Colin's surprise and fetched three plates to hide my mirth. He still wasn't used to the accuracy of dragon senses. Sure, they were muted when we were in our human bodies, but they were still quite a bit better than those of the average human. He'd learn, given time.

We waited with our question until Angie had served the stew.

"Lydia is worried about her grades in a few subjects," Colin started. "Would it be possible to get her a tutor?"

Feeling uncomfortable about laying the expense on Angie, I interrupted him. "I know it'll be expensive, but maybe we can use a little bit of my parents' hoard for it?" I made it sound like a question since I wasn't sure if dragon society allowed such a use of hoards. I held my breath.

"I think that's a great idea," Angie said, then flinched. A fraction of a second later, the backdoor opened and three members of the Council stepped in.

"I do not think so." Their leader was a middle-aged woman with long black hair that flowed freely over slender shoulders and very dark eyes. She shot Colin a piercing look. "There is no need for Her Majesty to learn anything concerning humans. Her place is with the dragons."

I stood up, pressed my palms on the tabletop, bent forward, and glared at her. "I will not be your queen."

Nicole walked through the mall like a spy on a mission. Her gaze darted everywhere, lingering longingly on the bookshop's window for a moment before she turned to scan the crowds for Harm, Lydia or her brother. She knew they always went to get an ice cream after school and she didn't fancy bumping into them. But she had promised Isabella she'd meet her by the fountain at three and it was already five minutes to. She hurried on as fast as she could. There; the fountain sparkled like a glittering display of diamonds in the sunshine falling through the roof. Just through the corridor past the toilets and she'd be there. She relaxed somewhat; still two minutes to go.

A hand pressed on her mouth and she was dragged backward. Instantly her heart raced. She wanted to shout, '*Someone, anyone, call the police*', but the corridor was empty. Despite struggling with all her might, her attacker dragged her through a service door. Panicked, she bit into the hand over her mouth, and when the fingers were jerked away, she managed to get one scream out. A shower of sparks hit the floor. She glanced up. The lamp sparked some more, throwing fiery electricity on the man.

He swore and slammed her into a wall. All the air was knocked from her. Tears shot into her eyes, and her heart cramped. Now she'd die! But where had the electricity come from?

Her legs refused to carry her any longer, and she slid down into a sitting position.

"Stop struggling." The man bent over her, the eyes behind the mask two narrow slits. He grabbed her wrists and tied them together with a shoelace. Despite her rapidly beating heart, Nicole tried to commit as many details of him to memory as she could, in the unlikely event that she survived and had to describe him to the police.

From the smoothness of his movements, he must be young. And fit, considering his build. His eyes were gray, and he smelled of peppermint. He was wearing a black shirt, black jeans, and black sneakers. With each blink of her eyes, she took in a different detail. It was as if her mind had turned into a camera that recorded more than just pictures. She felt absolutely certain that she could recall the man down to the color of his shoelaces.

"Don't move." He sat on his haunches. "And don't talk or I'll put some tape over your mouth."

She stared at him with wide eyes.

"Will you listen?"

She nodded.

"Good." His eyes looked less angry. "I'm sorry I had to kidnap you like this, but I need information."

"In… in… in…" She just didn't manage to push the word past the icy lump in her throat.

"Where is the dragon village?"

Dragons? Am I completely surrounded by insane people? Nicole pressed the palms of her hands against her eyes. "No, no, no, no. Dragons don't exist. I swear."

"I saw you fraternizing with one of them." The man didn't budge. "And I need to know where they live."

"I never met a dragon in my life." Nicole tried to sound convincing. She wouldn't betray her own insanity by admitting to something so ridiculous.

"You—" The man's head shot up. He stood, opened the maintenance door a crack, swore, and slipped through.

"I'm here!" Nicole yelled at the top of her lungs. "Help me!"

The door swung open and Harm entered, sniffing the air like a hunting dog. "Nicole?" His eyes widened and he was beside Nicole with a single stride. With bare fingers he ripped the shoelace apart as if it were nothing but paper. "What happened?"

"Oh, Harm." Nicole threw her arms around his neck. More sparks rained down from the lamp above, singeing Harm's beloved black leather jacket. Now he smelled of burnt leather and chewing gum. His dark hair tickled in her nose, but for once she felt safe. "Everyone is going crazy. That man …" Her voice trailed off. Should she admit that the man had been asking about dragons? Surely not. It'd only set off Harm and Colin again, and maybe Lydia too. Dragons weren't real. "We need to see the police," she said, determination in her voice.

"Fine." Harm helped her up. "I'll come with you."

Harm walked up to the front door of Colin and Nicole's house. Never in his life had he felt as insecure as right now. His knees trembled, and his heart beat as fast as if he'd raced a train and won. *Strange,* he thought. *It's as if something is draining my strength away. Surely I'm not afraid of Nicole, am I?* The finger he extended to press the doorbell trembled and his legs seemed too tired to carry him much longer. What if Nicole refused his offer? At the police station last night she'd clung to his hand as if he was the only stable point in the universe. But that didn't mean she'd like what he had to tell her. She was dead set against the idea that dragons existed; she'd completely pushed their existence out of her mind.

"Harm! What a nice surprise." Colin held the door open. "Come in."

"We need to talk," Harm said. "And when we're finished, I'll need to see your sister. Is she in?" He knew she was. He could smell her flowery body odor all the way down from her room, but he wanted to seem as human as possible for the moment.

"Sure. What do you want to talk about?" Colin led him upstairs into his bedroom, which was uncomfortably close to Nicole's.

Harm followed him, fighting the wobbly feeling in his legs. "Can she hear us?"

"No. She's listening to some music. Said she needed to clear her head."

Ah! A good exercise, Harm thought. "It seems she instinctively knows what's helpful for her."

"What are you talking about?" Colin frowned and plopped down on the bed.

Harm sat on a patch of the floor that wasn't covered in dirty laundry. To his surprise a wave of exhaustion threatened to overwhelm him. He was glad he no longer had to stand. He fought down the nausea with a couple of deep breaths before he spoke. "When I came to school the first day, I suspected it, but I'm absolutely certain now that Nicole is a witch."

Colin's jaw dropped, and he stared at Harm.

Harm hurried to explain. "At first it was only a hint with the tingling in my hand whenever I touched her. But yesterday, when she was attacked by that stranger—"

"She was attacked?" Colin sat up, eyes even wider. "She never said a word about that."

"Well, the situation was a little uncomfortable for her since the attacker had asked about the whereabouts of the dragons' settlement, and she just didn't want to admit it. She only told the police officer when he threatened to fine her for obstructing their investigation. Naturally he laughed at the notion of the existence of dragons. They're considering the incident an attack by a lunatic or drug addict, but I'm sure it's something different." Harm balled his hands into fists, a little worried that the strength he usually felt seemed to be missing. It was as if someone had doused some of the fire inside of him. Still, his anger burned, not as bright as it normally would but with a steady flame. "And if I get my hands on that guy I'll rip him apart. But right now I've come because Nicole defended herself in a rather unusual fashion. She used magic to make the lights rain electrical sparks down on the stranger."

"But ... magic?" Colin looked skeptical. "It could have been a broken lamp."

"I'm a magical creature. Believe me, I know when someone's using magic." Harm folded his arms in front of his chest, fighting another spell of dizziness. "Nicole needs to learn to control her powers. The magic she'd leaked yesterday could destroy her if she doesn't acknowledge it soon. An untrained witch is a danger to herself and her surroundings."

"But where did she get it? Girls don't become witches overnight, do they?"

Colin's questions were understandable even though Harm had no answer. As far as he knew, the few witches who'd emigrated to the States had been killed during the Salem witch trials. To his knowledge, not a single one had survived. He shrugged. "It doesn't really matter, does it? She is a witch and needs to learn to control her powers. How do we go about it?"

"I don't know." Colin seemed much paler than usual. Harm had noticed a few worry lines during the last few days, and sometimes Colin was rather absent-minded, but this was a new level of concern, albeit an understandable one.

Colin spoke hesitantly. "Maybe Angie is wrong and we should talk more with her whether she wants to or nor. We could take her to the forest and show her that dragons exist."

"It's not feasible. She's not ready to face us yet. We'd have to kidnap her, and that's something I won't allow," Harm said. After a long silence, he had an idea. "What if I give her a book about magic? She used to love books, and it reads like a scientific non-fiction book."

"She put away everything that's even remotely connected to fantasy and magic." Colin scratched the little stubble at his chin that might one day turn into a beard. "We'd have to make it look as if it is legitimate research."

"What do you propose?" Harm cocked his head, blinking away his tiredness.

"Well, we must make her believe that our history teacher wants her to do a presentation on the belief in magic in the Middle Ages and during the modern-era witch hunts. She's always done extra work to get good grades."

"If she likes doing extra work, Lydia can order her with the Queen's Voice." Harm suddenly felt much more upbeat.

"She can?" Colin slid to the bed's edge. "But why doesn't she simply order her to believe in dragons again?"

Icy dread flooded through Harm's veins. "Queen's Orders are irreversible, and sometimes they break people. If Lydia would order Nicole to so something she's absolutely determined not to do, it might kill your sister."

"Oh…" Colin's voice trailed off. After a while he said, "In that case the idea with the extra homework is a really good one, I think."

"I think so too. And when Lydia's done, I'll smuggle 'The Science of Magic' into Nicole's backpack. I'm close to her most of the time anyway. She needs protecting. Especially from those girls."

"Girls?" Colin's eyebrows rose again.

"She's been hanging out with Isabella and her pals." Harm shrugged. "I don't understand what she sees in them. They treat her like crap unless I'm there. Then they're all over me, batting their eyelashes and smiling false smiles."

"Oh, those." Colin nodded. "They've been after me too, but I refused to be one of their countless ex-boyfriends. I wonder why Nicole bothers."

"Maybe she's missing us more than she cares to admit." Harm bit his tongue, appalled by the longing in his voice and the hole in his heart. Was that the reason he felt so weak?

"Maybe she is."

Harm got up. "Shall I talk to her right now, or shall we fetch Lydia first?"

"Let's fetch Lydia." Colin's voice held the same tone of longing Harm had experienced just a moment ago. It wasn't possible that he was interested in Nicole, or was it? No—falling for a witch was way too dangerous. He'd have to take better care of his heart.

When they descended the stairs, another wave of exhaustion rolled over Harm and the world went dark.

He came to pretty quickly, curled up at the bottom of the stairs with a burning pain in his right leg. Through the open front door he could see the flashing of a blue light, but its meaning didn't register until two men in orange clothes with reflectors crouched beside him and prodded his neck, his arms, his belly, and every other part of his body, talking gibberish.

"I need an IV and a stiff neck." A third orange-clad man hurried out, and the man at Harm's side turned to Colin. "Can you tell us what happened, sir?" He touched Harm's leg.

Colin's answer was drowned out by Harm's howl. How could this have happened? Did Colin see how weak he had been, or would he put the fall down to an accident?

"Leave me alone." He struggled to sit up. "I'm fine."

"Can you please alert a parent or legal guardian? We'll take him to Community General." Speaking to Colin, the orange man pushed Harm back easily, and he didn't have the strength to resist. A sudden worry flushed through him. Why was he so weak? He should be able to wipe the floor with this human. If Colin hadn't realized how weak he was, he must have noticed it now. Tears filled his eyes, but he swallowed them, pretending everything was fine. He forced himself to relax so the paramedics could do their job. When they wheeled him into the ambulance, he reached for Colin and whispered, "You should have called Angie. She'd be much better at helping me."

"I'll tell her where you are."

Harm watched Colin's drawn face until the doors thumped shut and the ambulance started to move. Then he closed his eyes and allowed the weariness to wash away his consciousness.

FOURTH CHAPTER

$\mathcal{I}$ stared at the ceiling of my room, not really seeing it. My mind was too troubled. In a few more minutes, Angie would call me downstairs for an official Council meeting, and I hated it when the Council visited. Every time they put more pressure on me to return with them as their queen. If only Colin were here with me, but he hadn't been around yesterday—football training—and for today Angie had told him to stay away. My dull anger had subsided pretty quickly. It was better for him not to be forced to sit through a Council meeting, no matter how much I needed him.

Thinking of him warmed me through and through.

"Honey, don't you think it's time to acknowledge who you are?" Mother's voice spoke right in my mind, filling me with a similar warmth as my thoughts of Colin.

Father added, "We know the temptations of the human world, and understand. However, you've also got a duty to our race. They count on you since you are our only heir."

"I know." A black cloud swallowed my heart. Why did I have to be born a dragon? Why couldn't Colin have been born one? If we'd been of the same species, everything would have been so much easier.

"Lydia?" Angie's voice carried through the house even though she could have called me with a dragon's growl that no one but dragons and elephants could hear. So, she preferred human methods too. Reluctantly I got up and went downstairs. The short distance down the stairs, through the hall, and into the living room felt like a marathon. With every step, the weight on my shoulders grew.

"We'll be with you, regardless of what you decide." Mother's voice eased my fear.

"Find a balance between your needs and those of your species," Father suggested. How could I do that if they shot down every single one of my arguments?

"Your Majesty!" Four women and three men sank to their knees and lowered their heads. Only Angie remained standing. She nodded to the place at the head of the living room table, but I steered right to the sofa. I would not take the chair. It'd be too much of a symbol. "Thank you for coming," I said, although I really longed to tell them to go to hell.

When they realized that I would not sit at the table, the Council fetched chairs to sit in a circle around the sofa. Only Angie dared to sit beside me on the sofa. I was glad she was so close.

A slender woman with long dark tresses stood up, bowed to me, and spoke. "As the Head of Council of Her Majesty Lydia Concordia Draconia Dragonis, I hereby declare this meeting opened."

My anger flared up. "I am not your queen yet."

"We're here to discuss that," the Head of Council said.

"So, why did you open the meeting in my name?" I glared at her with balled fists despite Angie's hand on my arm. Still, I felt its soothing effect. My anger already died down. We did have to find a way to make this work for everybody.

"I am sorry, Your Majesty." The Head of Council bowed once more. "However, when a member of the royal family is in attendance, I cannot lawfully open a meeting of the Council as Regent of the Realm. I'd be a traitor. But we all are aware that this is a special meeting, and that the traditional opening formula is not binding until your coronation."

"But I don't want a coronation." What a pity that stomping my foot would have been considered childish. I felt like it. "And I don't want to be a dragon all the time. I want to explore my human side. With Colin."

"Ah, yes, we'll be getting to him later," one of the men said. His pale face and stooped shoulders gave the impression that he wasn't seeing much of the sun. "But first things first. Are the King and Queen with you?"

I frowned. Why did they want to know? But then I shrugged and told them the truth. "They've been with me ever since the accident. It just took me a while to realize."

The man nodded. "Very well. In that case we'll simply return to the old reign." He said a word that reverberated through me. My whole body seemed to expand and become semi-transparent. A white-golden light grew in size with my body. It hurt. Someone was pulling me apart as if I was nothing but an insect.

Father roared.

Another dragon roared.

Mother's warm light encompassed me and pulled me back together. Her voice carried through the house and—I was fairly certain of it, although I didn't have proof—through the heads

46

of all the dragons in America. "Like every queen-to-be, our daughter has the right to choose her own way. We will oppose anyone who tries to take that right away from her."

The light got sucked back into me, pulling all my scattered body parts back together. Panting and with a thundering heart, I sat on the sofa and stared at the pale man. He'd slumped and looked like a heap of laundry as he was lying there on the ground before me.

"Drat." The Head of Council looked at the remaining Council members. "Does anyone know why he tried this?"

Silence.

As I studied the pale faces, I was pretty sure that this attack had surprised them just as much as me. I relaxed a little, and all of a sudden I realized Angie was holding me tight. Her arms squeezed me so strongly, I found it hard to breathe. I turned to her, swallowing a lump in my throat when I noticed the tears in her eyes. "You can let go now," I whispered, but because of the silence, it sounded as if I'd screamed.

Angie flinched but let go. She blinked away the tears. "I'd heard about a restoration spell but thought it'd been lost in ancient times."

"He was our head librarian," a wrinkled and tanned crone said. "If someone was able to find a long-lost spell, it would have been him. What a loss." The gaze she shot me wasn't exactly friendly. "And all that just because a selfish fledgling doesn't honor the duty of her blood."

"Duty of her blood. Bullshit!"

I'd never, ever heard Angie use an expletive like this. Shocked, I held my breath, just like all the other dragons. Only when she kept speaking did I realize that she'd used the word deliberately to shock the others into silence. That way she was the one everybody had to listen to.

"All of you know that an emerging queen has the right to abdicate any time and for any reason before her coronation. Just like every female sibling of an emerging queen has the right to challenge her for the throne. Just because our emerging queen doesn't have any siblings, can't mean we'll ignore our own traditions. This attack," she pointed at the librarian at her feet, "needs to be investigated in full. So far Lydia has only seen the dark and nasty sides of dragon culture—our rage and anger, our difficulty to find a compromise, our struggles with flexibility. Two dragons even tried to kill her just because they had different ideas about how our community should be ruled." She paused for breath and tried a winning smile. "Let us show Lydia how wonderful it is to be a dragon. Let her see the love we feel, not just for our own tribe but for all of dragonkind. Let her participate in our celebrations and share our joy about a hatching. I'm quite sure that the more she'll re-learn about us, the harder it will become for her to refuse your request."

Yeah, I thought. *Go ahead and make it really hard on me. But that won't work. Not as long as you don't accept Colin as my mate.*

"What do you suggest?" Angie sat down again and nodded to the Head of Council, who took over from there.

"Well, isn't there some free time in a human child's schedule that she could spend with us?" One of the younger females blushed when everybody turned to her. "I just thought I'd read that somewhere."

"It's not far to spring break." I couldn't believe I said that. Was I really considering visiting the dragons in their remote village? What about Colin? It'd rip my heart out of my chest if

I had to leave without him. And Nicole? We still hadn't found a way to convince her my species existed.

"Come on," Angie urged. "Jump in on this. It's a start, and the more you show her, the more likely it is she'll enjoy being a dragon."

"What about that ... *human*, she's so fond of?" The only remaining man in the Council spat out the word as if it were an insult.

My mouth opened of its own accord to protest, but I snapped it closed. We were trying to find a peaceful solution, after all.

"Colin will have to come. Lydia bonded with him," Angie said, and a collective gasp went through the Council.

"But there was no bonding ceremony," the young woman said.

Angie smiled at her. "As little as you like it, some things can happen without ceremonies."

"Well." A middle-aged woman stood up. "I'm willing to take in any human that accompanies my queen. If they're good enough for her, they'll be good enough for me."

"What about Mordekay's son?" Unblinking, the Head of Council stared at Angie. "After all you've told us about Mordekay's plot, no one will take him in."

"He isn't Mordekay's son." I explained the situation. "I'm sure he'll like to stay here to take care of his father."

"And if not, he can stay in my house," Angie said. "I trust him."

An invigorated discussion broke out. Everybody spoke to somebody at the same time. I pressed my hands over my ears and let the cacophony run its course. It seemed dragons really were inflexible. And it seemed they loved discussions. When the arguments went in circles, I even napped a bit, but eventually the talking died down.

Angie summed up the decision. "So we all agree that Lydia will visit our main village as soon as the spring break starts, and she may bring Harm, Colin, and Nicole if they want to come."

A few Council members grumbled, but the majority nodded their heads. From deep down inside of me, a warmth spread outward that told me how much my parents approved of this compromise. I put on my best smile and dismissed the Council.

Barely two minutes later the last member had gone, taking the dead librarian with him.

"Well, all things considered, this was a successful meeting, don't you think?" Angie grinned at me.

I smiled back, secure in the knowledge that my parents had once more protected me. "I just hope there won't be any more assassination attempts. It would ruin spring break."

Fifth Chapter

*F*ighting boredom, Harm let the humans run their tests on his injured leg. They declared it broken and put it into a plaster. Why that was necessary, he couldn't say. It was a clean break without complications. It'd heal in a fortnight. And the flimsy cast wouldn't last a day.

"You will need a lot of rest. No sports, no driving, no kinky sex." The doctor grinned as if he'd made a joke.

Harm frowned. Should he have understood?

The doctor's smile wavered, but he spoke on. "In four weeks we'll see how well the healing progresses and maybe get started on rehab. You should be back with your football team long before the summer."

"Summer? What about spring break?" Harm's head whirled. Spring break was only four weeks away. Didn't the doctor know that dragon bones healed a lot faster than human bones?

"As I said, a lot of rest." The doctor scribbled something into the folder he was holding. "Someone will be with you in a minute." He left the room through the sliding door just as Blackfeather in his Smolinsky guise entered.

"Are you alright?" His obvious worry caught Harm off guard. He growled and frowned. "I'm fine. Leave me alone."

"The doctor said they'd keep you here until tomorrow." Blackfeather walked closer to the bed, his hands behind his back. "Is there anything I can do for you?"

"Why would they keep me? My leg's broken, not my neck."

A smile flickered over Smolinsky's face. "They need to make sure you don't have a concussion."

"I'm a dragon." Harm slid his feet over the edge of the flat, uncomfortable bed in the examination room. The one in the cast seemed to weigh a ton. "I don't get concussions."

Just as he got up, a burly orderly entered with a wheelchair. His teeth shone like snow in his friendly, dark face. "Let's get you to bed, pal."

Harm pushed aside his helping hand and set his feet down. Immediately the room whirled around him. If the orderly hadn't caught him, he would have fallen again. *Why am I so weak?* He couldn't think of a time when this had ever happened before. Was he ill after all? He allowed the orderly to pick him up and place him into the wheelchair.

"We've got a nice, soft bed for you, pal." The man grabbed the handles and pushed. Blackfeather opened the door for him. Harm closed his eyes, fighting dizziness. Maybe it wasn't such a bad idea to lie down after all.

After he was safely tucked into a bed in a room that smelled of disinfectant and overcooked food, Blackfeather pulled a chair closer and sat down. He didn't look at Harm when he spoke. "You do know that it takes a human six to eight weeks to heal a broken bone, right?"

Harm shook his head, cleared his throat, and said, "Really? That long?"

"To keep your disguise credible, you'll have to follow doctor's orders, and that means no football."

"Hey!" Harm sat up straight. "I just learned the rules properly and the coach wanted to put me on the team for the next game."

"I'm sorry." Smolinsky's features resembled those of a beagle. "We've either got to find a different subject for you, or you must return to the village. The Council would prefer the latter option."

"I'm not leaving Lydia." Harm glared at Smolinsky. *Or Nicole.* "She needs me more than she wants to admit. And Colin isn't strong enough to counter an attack on Lydia." *Or Nicole.*

"I know." Smolinsky got up. "I'll arrange for a transfer."

"What subject will I get instead?"

"Whatever is available." Smolinsky bent forward as if to hug Harm, but instead took his hand and shook it. "I'll pick you up tomorrow after school."

He left without looking back, and Harm wondered whether Blackfeather liked him at all. Not that he'd been used to get a lot of positive emotions from Mordekay, but Blackfeather topped the aloofness by another margin. *He's my father, for crying out loud. Why can't he at least hug me? Angie does it all the time.* His heart rubbed like a stone in his chest. He blinked away his tears and leaned back into his cushion. Maybe Blackfeather just needed more time. Surely he was just as unused to being a father as Harm was to being a son worthy of risking one's life for. He had just thought that after nearly dying for his son, there'd be … he didn't know what, but shouldn't there be … more?

Maybe he should talk to someone about this, but who'd be suitable? Lydia? No. She had too many problems of her own. Nicole? His heart contracted painfully. She wouldn't listen to him. The minute he mentioned dragons, she'd be running as if he were the devil. And Colin would probably not understand.

He pondered the problem until his eyes drooped and sleep claimed him.

The morning in the hospital proved to be extremely boring for Harm. Since he didn't experience complications at night, he was to be released as soon as Blackfeather could pick him up. After the talk with the doctor, who pointed out once more that he should get rest, no one looked in on him. The nurses were too busy and his friends were still in school. All Harm could do was to think. And his mind did its best to make him as miserable as possible.

Surely Colin would stop being his friend after witnessing his weakness. Why hadn't he been able to keep it together just a little longer? He could have rested at home. Why did he have to fall down the stairs and break his leg?

And Nicole would certainly never, ever accept that there were dragons and witches. She'd move away, maybe blowing up herself and some part of the world where he couldn't help her.

Lydia would refuse the crown and dragonkind would slip into an all-out war, destroying each other. Blackfeather would be the first to die, as uncomfortable as he was with his new dragon side.

The scenarios his mind showed him became more and more unrealistic and wild. A big lump grew in his chest, forcing tears into his eyes. Caught in a vortex of despair, Harm blinked them back as best he could. Just as Mordekay's black face rose from the vortex, snarling at him, the door opened and Lydia looked in.

"Here you are." Her smile brightened the room. "You'd think a hospital would know where they put their patients. They sent us to three different rooms."

"And it's a maze," Colin said. "Did you know you can't reach the west wing from the main building directly?"

Harm's eyes widened. They were still his friends? Didn't they mind his weakness?

"We offered to pick you up to save Blackfeather from driving a car. He's not very used to that." Lydia picked up the crutches that were leaning against the wall. "And we brought a surprise."

The door opened once more.

"Hi Harm." Nicole stared at the ground, clearly wavering between fleeing and entering. Her red hair glowed in the light from the window and Harm's heart caught fire. Delighted, he drank in every single freckle in her face. A lump stuck in his throat that he couldn't talk past. Nicole looked up. "I'm sorry I've been so distant the last few months."

He wanted to say, "That's okay," but not a word managed to squeeze past the lump.

"Come on," Colin said. "Time to go home. Anyone in for an ice cream on the way back?"

"I'm game." Lydia handed Harm the crutches.

Nicole hesitated, then looked at her brother. "Only if you keep your promise." Her face was drawn, and Harm's heart contracted painfully in sympathy. Staring at Colin, she said, "No talk about dragons."

"As promised." Colin bowed like an old-fashioned courtier and held the door open for everyone.

Half an hour later they were sitting at their favorite table in the mall's ice cream parlor licking their favorite flavors in companionable silence, when Lydia fixed her gaze on Nicole.

"I've heard you're doing extra work for history?"

Harm felt the power of her voice. It was so strong that he longed to call the history teacher to ask for extra work too. He felt hot and cold by turns when he realized that this was the time for their plan. Why then did it feel so wrong to use magic on Nicole?

"Oh yes." Nicole's face lit up. "We're doing the witch hunts right now and I've got to find out what kind of superstitions people at that time believed. And then I'm to compare them with accounts of today's witches."

"Sounds interesting." Harm tried his best to seem pleased for her. It nearly tore his heart to know how they were deceiving her. Was this really necessary?

"I'll be able to read again." Nicole's smile was a little unsure. "I'm sure non-fiction won't..." Her voice trailed off.

At the same time, Colin's mobile beeped. He glanced at it and burst out laughing. "Do you know which course Blackfeather organized for you as football replacement? It's the only one that doesn't clash with your other courses."

Harm's eyebrows rose but he didn't stop licking his ice cream to answer. Considering Colin's mirth, he'd tell him anyway.

"You're in drama class." Ice cream dropped from his spoon onto the table he was laughing so hard.

"Isabella said they're doing an adaptation of Pete's Dragon." Nicole grinned, but to Harm's surprise her eyes remained sad.

"You should play the dragon, Harm," Lydia said.

"No talk about dragons," Harm reminded her. Still, he was worried and also a little angry. Drama meant acting, didn't it? And acting was like living a lie. He'd never lied in his whole life. Dragons were incapable of direct lying. What had Blackfeather thought when he put him into an acting class? Had he thought at all? Mordekay would never have selected a class like that. Wasn't there a subject more suitable for a dragon?

"Calm down. You're smoking already." Lydia's hand touched his arm and her voice spoke in his mind. He flinched. It was the first time ever someone spoke to him this way.

"Yes, Your Majes—"

"DON'T you dare!" Her mind voice sounded like molten lava filled with a command he couldn't ignore. "Never call me 'Majesty'. I'll always be Lydia for you."

"Sorry, Lydia. I'm not used to mind-talk. Mordekay locked my brain against the other dragons."

"I know. I had to dismantle some of the defenses he put up." He could feel her smile deep inside. "I left some so you won't get swamped when you visit the other dragons."

"Thank you."

Nicole waved her hands in front of Harm's face. "What are you staring at? Did I dribble ice cream all over me?"

"No! You're just so beautiful." He blinked and noticed that Nicole's jaw had dropped. Heat shot through Harm. Had he really said that?

Oblivious to the strained silence, or intentionally ignoring it, Colin said, "Drama class isn't half bad. Even if you don't know how to act, you can always do something else to help." He chuckled. "Like sewing costumes or painting scenery."

"Yeah, and that's so much better for a macho man like him," Nicole countered, but there was a twinkle in her eyes.

Still feeling way too hot, Harm returned his gaze to his ice cream and attacked the melting mess with a vengeance, listening to the friendly banter between the others.

A few days later, Harm hobbled along the corridor to drama class, biting his lip. Did he really have to go alone? At least Colin could have come. On the other hand, he wasn't a hatchling anymore who needed his hand held for new experiences. And Mordekay had trained him to fit in, so maybe this wasn't as bad as he feared. But when he saw Isabella and Chelsea standing in the doorway to the classroom, he knew it would be worse.

"Harm!" Isabella batted her eyelashes and grabbed his arm, obstructing the use of his crutch. "Let me help you."

If he wanted to use the crutch, he'd have to remove the girl bodily. Harm shuddered. Regardless how annoying those girls were, it wouldn't do to become violent.

"Are you nuts?" A dark-haired teenager grabbed Isabella's arm and pulled her off Harm. He glared at her. "Are you trying to get him off balance so he'll break the other leg too?"

"I'm not talking to freaks." Isabella stuck up her nose and marched past Harm's savior. Chelsea followed her wordlessly. The door slammed behind her.

"Why are they calling you a freak?" Harm stared at the boy beside him. He didn't have extra arms or green skin or antennae. He frowned.

"Straight-A student in all subjects, that's me." The youth grinned, and his eyes sparkled mischievously.

"They call someone a freak who likes to know things?" Harm shook his head. *I'll never understand humans.*

"Who cares?" The teen pushed his glasses higher and studied Harm from head to toe.

Shifting uncomfortably under the scrutiny, Harm cleared his throat. "Ehm. Thanks for the rescue."

"Those girls are a nuisance, aren't they?" He held out a hand. "I'm Luke, by the way." When he realized that Harm couldn't shake hands, he blushed and turned to open the door again.

Holding it, he added, "I've heard you had an accident. What a pity. You were one of the coach's greatest hopes."

"Are you a football fan?" Hobbling forward, Harm found it strange how many people seemed to know him even though he'd never met them before.

"Only of our high school team." Luke closed the door behind them silently.

Harm allowed his eyes to adjust to the semi-darkness of the theater. The windowless room was surprisingly big. On the side where they had entered, piles of canvas frames were leaning against the wall. The ground's smooth, pale parquet went all the way to the front of the stage where the group of students huddling around the teacher seemed a little lost. Behind them, Harm noticed several rows of seating. *It's a real theater.* His surprise couldn't have been bigger. He'd expected a normal classroom. "Wow, this is…" His voice faltered.

"Impressive, isn't it?" Luke grinned. "But it's nothing compared to the reconstructed Globe Theatre in London. Ever been there?"

Harm shook his head.

"If you get the chance, look at it. It's fascinating."

"I'm not really into theaters." Harm moved toward the front of the stage where the other students were waiting.

"Me neither." Luke stayed close to him. "I'm more of a science fan, but my biggest hobby is dragons. Have you ever read Dragonology by Peter Dickinson? Or 'Das geheime Handbuch der Drachenkunde'? They're both great books to start out with."

He babbled on, but Harm didn't listen any more. Unbelieving, he stopped and stared at the slender youth. There were books about dragons? Books that humans read? Did they say anything about the village? His mouth opened and closed with the questions whirling through his mind.

When Luke noticed Harm wasn't moving any longer, he turned and cocked his head with a frown. "Oh, come on." His voice sounded annoyed. "Don't be as inflexible as Isabella. Just because I believe in dragons, doesn't mean I'm a freak. It's just a hobby. And anyways, 'There are more things in heaven and earth, Horatio, than are dreamed of in your philosophy.'"

Harm shook his head and blurted out the first question that came to his mind. "Who on earth is Horatio?"

Luke laughed and began a lengthy explanation about an author named Shakespeare who wrote the play 'Hamlet' he'd quoted. The way he told the story, it could as well have been true. Could it be that he didn't make any difference between his fantasies and reality? Maybe his dragon research was make-believe. Harm would have to investigate.

"How much longer are the two of you going to dawdle?" the teacher called. Isabella and Chelsea giggled, but the other students only turned friendly, open faces toward Harm. He began to hobble forward again. *This might turn out to be great move after all,* he thought.

Sixth Chapter

When Nicole set out for the bus, Isabella and her pals stopped her with their arms akimbo.

"Why didn't you tell us Harm would be coming to drama class?" Isabella's tone was unfriendly. "We could have brought some sweets."

"Yeah, and we could have looked on the internet to find out how to treat a crippled patient," Patricia said past her chewing gum.

"Harm isn't crippled." Nicole tried to get past them. "And he doesn't much care for sweets."

"He's always in the ice cream parlor with Colin and his slut," Chelsea said.

Lydia is no slut, Nicole wanted to scream; instead she ground her teeth. "If you don't mind, I've got a bus to catch."

"Oh, no driving license yet?" Isabella's smile was a sneer. "Well, your problem. You're not going anywhere right now until you've told us everything you know about Harm."

The three girls surrounded Nicole, and she wouldn't be able to break free without hurting someone. She pressed her lips together. *Harm and Lydia are most definitely better friends,* she thought. *Maybe I should be more lenient with their antics. Many people believe in dragons.*

"What's his favorite food?" Isabella bent forward until her nose nearly touched Nicole's. "What's his favorite color? What kind of girlfriend is he looking for? Long term, short term?"

"What hair color does he prefer?" Patricia fell in. "And what hairstyle, long or short? What about makeup—pale, rosy or tanned? Which TV shows does he like? What's his favorite actor?"

"And just how much pocket money does he get?" Chelsea chimed in.

Nicole had tried to get a word in edgewise, but the girls went on with questions that became increasingly more uncomfortable for her.

"Does he like sex?" Isabella seemed eager. "How many women did he already have? And would he mind the woman being on top?"

"You're not a woman yet." Nicole knew she didn't want to know the answers to Isabella's questions.

"I am. Ask Robert Delaney."

"And anyway," Nicole went on without waiting for the girls to start another tirade of questions, "I don't know the answers to your questions."

"Well, find them out." Isabella balled her right hand to a fist and held it under Nicole's nose. "And hurry or we'll find a way to get the answers out of you regardless."

"In that case you'd have to let me catch the bus Harm normally takes too, won't you?" It gave Nicole great satisfaction to defeat Isabella without lifting a finger, especially since she knew that Harm had left an hour earlier today.

With an angry glare the other girl stepped aside and let her pass. Nicole stepped out of the circle and hurried toward the waiting bus. She felt the girls' stares in her back like daggers. Why was she trying so hard not to annoy them? She really should get back to her old friends. It would be so great if she didn't have to be friendly to Isabella and her pals any longer. If only Lydia, Harm, and Colin wouldn't insist dragons were real. What if their talk triggered another hallucination? Life was complicated enough without them.

She found a spare seat and sat down just as her mobile rang. "Yes?"

"Ehem … Hi Nicole." The voice triggered a shower of sparks all over her body. "It's Harm. Colin says he's got to … I mean … we're going to the mall again this afternoon, but he can't come. Would you mind if I picked you up? We might have a guest. His name's Luke and he's extremely bright. Colin thinks he might be a good tutor for Lydia."

"Is she coming too?" Nicole held her breath.

"I'm sure she will." Harm sounded a little worried, as if he didn't know for sure. "But Colin meant to talk to Luke without her first."

Nicole hesitated. Did she dare meet with him?

"I've got a book for your presentation, too."

Was he really begging? A smile spread over her face. In that case the question was, did he beg because he didn't want to eat his ice cream alone, or was he truly interested in her company? Well, that was easy to test.

"I had been thinking about a walk in the woods." She smiled even though Harm couldn't see her.

"I'd love that."

Her heart missed a beat.

"I'll pick you up in an hour, if that's okay?"

"That's fine by me." Nicole ended the call and pressed the mobile to her chest. What had she done? Was she inviting insanity into her life? But Harm had sounded so ... so ... well, *caring* wasn't the right word ... but maybe ... concerned?

Daydreaming, she rode home and nearly missed her stop.

Pacing up and down the living room, Nicole waited for Harm's arrival. He was right on time, hobbling along the sidewalk toward her house. Hobbling? Why hadn't he come by car? How would they get to the woods without a car?

When she asked him, his answer was, "I haven't finished my driving license yet. Since Colin has a license, I thought you could drive too."

"Colin's thrifty. I spent too much money on books." She smiled. "But maybe he can take us before he goes wherever he needs to be."

Luckily Colin was still in the house and willing to help. "But I'll be gone for two or three hours minimum," he said.

"That's fine. The weather is nice and we've got warm jackets." On a whim, Nicole hugged her brother. "Thanks."

A little while later, he dropped them at the familiar parking lot. Nicole looked around and shivered. It had probably not been the best idea to come here again.

Hugging herself, she asked. "Can we use a path we haven't used before?"

"Sure." Harm took a few tentative steps toward a forest road. "I'm supposed to go easy. And anyway, it needs to be wide enough so I won't get stuck."

His grin was infectious. She caught up with him, and they walked side by side through the woods. At first Nicole didn't know what she should talk about, but then she remembered the girls' silly questions. Maybe they'd leave her some room if she brought them Harm's answers. "Would you mind me asking some questions Isabella and her pals are pestering me about?"

"Those three drive me crazy." Harm snorted, then shrugged as best was possible with crutches. "But if it helps you … go ahead."

She started with the general questions and learned that Harm loved green, Mozart, dark clothes, and more or less raw steaks. He answered in a friendly tone, smiling at her a lot, so she gathered her courage and asked the one thing the three girls probably had the biggest interest in.

Harm's answer was crystal clear. "No, I haven't gotten a girlfriend yet, but I'll not allow either of the three to claim a place in my heart."

"They won't like to hear that." She had to admit that his answer calmed her heart. She hadn't even known it was beating so hard. What was wrong with her? They were walking at a snail's pace through the woods, not trying to run a marathon. Why then was she so flustered?

"Not my problem." Harm stared at the ground as if debating with himself. Then he continued. "The woman I'll give my heart to will need to accept me just the way I am. She can't be afraid of my," he hesitated a moment, but then plowed on, "my dragonish side, and she needs to be tolerant of all the things I don't know about human culture. Also, she needs to like reading, because that's something I enjoy too. And I want to be able to laugh with her, and experience adventures. She has to be there for me when I need her, regardless of what I did, and I'll always be there for her too. I want a girlfriend who is ready to spend the rest of her life with me."

Nicole's heart sped up again, and she didn't even mind the short mention of dragons.

"Oh, and it doesn't hurt if she's attractive, with freckles." Harm looked at her and winked.

She blushed. "I ... I'm ..." Clearing her throat, she changed the subject abruptly. "You said you'd have a book I could use for my presentation?"

"It's one of my father's. He's got quite a lot." He stopped, set down his backpack, and rummaged around in it. "It is ancient and from Europe."

"Won't your dad be angry if you lend it to me?"

"I asked for his permission." Harm pulled out a small, leather-bound book with a bluish stone laid into the front. The sides of the pages looked as if they'd been ripped rather than cut, and the paper itself seemed more yellow than white. There were two thin, long leather ribbons sewn into the back and the front of the book. They were wrapped around it and tied above the stone.

"You've got to be careful when you read it." He handed her the book. "I hope it'll be helpful. It contains a lot of the history of magic as they saw it back then. It's even got a few spells in it."

His voice held a tone of reverence that made Nicole hesitate.

She took the book but couldn't help teasing him. "Don't tell me you believe in witches."

He shrugged, and her face fell.

With more vehemence than she'd planned, she said, "Witches don't exist."

66

"Not any more. Not even in Europe." He sounded sad. "The witch hunts saw to that, and whoever they didn't burn was later murdered in WWII concentration camps."

Nicole's jaw fell. Did he really believe this?

"Harm, I ..." She didn't want to hurt his feelings, but she also couldn't let him deceive himself. Getting angry wouldn't help either, so she tried her most gentle voice. "There is no magic. Not in our world."

Since he was crouching to close his backpack, he looked up at her with a mischievous grin. "Why don't you prove it to me?"

"Harm!" Nicole frowned, not knowing whether he was trying to flirt with her or being serious.

"Oh, come on." Harm stood up and leaned on his crutches again. "What harm can it do? If there's no magic like you say, nothing will happen. And if there is magic, like I believe, you'll experience something wonderful." He pointed to a fallen tree trunk at the side of the road. "We could sit there and find a suitable spell. Come on. Let's be adventurous."

His smile was infectious, so she complied. He was right. What harm could it do? She sat down and waited until he had maneuvered himself beside her. The plaster on his leg didn't hinder him much, and she realized he must have quite the musculature to sit down so effortlessly despite his broken leg.

Blushing at her own thoughts, she opened the book and flipped through the pages. It was handwritten, but the letters were very different from what she was used to. It looked as if someone had filled the pages with thin, black scratches, side by side by side. She frowned. "I can't read this."

"Oh, right. I forgot." Harm bent closer to her. He smelled of soap and smoked leather. The scent made her lick her lips.

"Let's see. There is an index somewhere in the back. The author was rather advanced for his time."

With shaking fingers, she flipped to the end of the book. Harm read out the last page.

"Spelles, usefulle for the initiated. How to find a dragon, page 4."

"No dragons." Her voice sounded hoarse.

"Understood. Let's see. How to call a mermaid isn't much use in the woods either. What about this one?" He pointed to a line at the bottom. "How to create the illusion of a unicornus."

"That sounds promising." She looked at him. "And it won't work anyway."

"We'll see." Harm flipped the pages, and his arm brushed hers. She felt a heatwave burn through her coat. "Okay, this is what it says. Findeth a leafe of a birchen tree, it needes not be fresh. Crumple it between your fingeres and think of a unicornus. Fixeth the image in your mind and call out, 'Ranasolat prefesporil rasallah unicornus'. Well, that sounds straightforward and easy."

"If I can remember those words. They are really strange." Nicole shook her head. Why had she agreed to this?

Harm put a reassuring hand on her arm. "I've found that with magic, it's far more important to get the intent right. If the words differ slightly it shouldn't be such a big deal."

"So, you're an expert now, are you?" She tried to shake the uncomfortable feeling she'd had ever since Harm had read out the spell's words. They seemed to cling to her mind and she was unable to shake them. She just knew that she'd pronounce them right even if she'd never hear them again.

"Would you rather not do it?" There was a worry frown on his face, and it made her heart melt. Although this experiment obviously meant a lot to him, he was ready to give her a way out.

He was a great friend after all. Even if he did believe in magic and dragons. What was so wrong about that anyway? Nicole resolved to spend more time with her friends again from now on. They were tons better than Isabella, Chelsea, and Patricia or any other girl she'd met in school.

"No, let's get this out of the way once and for all." She forced herself to smile.

"Okay. Let's get started." He lifted himself up and propped the crutches under his arms again. "Let's find a leaf of a birch tree."

It took them quite a while to find one, although the white and black trunks were easily spotted. Even though the buds were swollen and ready to open, it wasn't spring yet, so they had to look at the ground. It was muddy since it'd been raining a lot lately, but eventually they found a yellow leaf that was mostly intact. Its heart shape with the serrated rim shone out from a patch of brown leaves as if someone had planted it there.

Nicole picked it up gingerly. She didn't really want to, somehow knowing that something would happen that she would not be able to undo. But Harm counted on her, and she needed to prove that there was no such thing as magic. *If I'm right he'll just say that I'm not a witch,* a nagging voice in her mind whispered. *And he'll go on and keep believing in all sorts of silly things.* She shook the voice off. "I'm ready."

"Me too." Harm looked at her steadily. His smile warmed her through and through. Blushing, she turned away and looked at her leaf. She crumpled it between her fingers, which proved to be harder than she had thought. The leaf was more leathery than brittle, but she did her best, and soon it was shredded. At the same time, she called up the picture she had in her mind of a unicorn. When she was sure that it was as perfect as she could get it, she called out the words that still clung to her mind.

Three things happened at once.

The words seemed to settle into a part of her brain that hadn't been used before. They purred and sent pleasurable shivers down her spine.

Harm gasped.

And a unicorn stepped from the underbrush.

Open-mouthed, Nicole stared at the delicate creature. It was barely bigger than a German Shepherd with a coat whiter than any snow she'd ever seen. A little beard hung from its chin, and its swishing tail ended in a pompom of longer hairs. But the most marvelous sight was its horn. Sparking like diamond dust, its pearl-colored radiance filled the woods with light.

Flowers shot out of the ground where it stood and burst into colorful blooms. Trees opened their buds, turning the world around them into a green oasis.

No! Nicole froze to the marrow. *That isn't possible. There is no magic.*

Seventh Chapter

"Wow." Harm spoke in a whisper. "It's the best illusion I've ever seen."

"Whom are you calling an illusion?" the unicorn asked, and Harm's jaw dropped. This most definitely was more than an illusion. With awe he looked at Nicole, who stood slack-jawed beside him. A wave of dizziness hit him. *Not now!* He pushed it aside as best he could.

"I have the distinct impression of being real," the unicorn said and took a step forward, making more of the woods burst into lush green. "The sweet maiden called me."

"Nooooo!" Nicole screamed, and the unicorn took a step back. Instinctively Harm closed his arms around Nicole. She flailed and screamed and pressed her eyes shut. Tears flooded her cheeks and soaked her jacket, and her legs buckled. Since Harm's strength had obviously stayed behind at the hospital, they sank to the ground arm in arm. She struggled so hard, he needed all his agility to hold her.

"What is wrong with the young lady?" The unicorn stepped closer again.

Harm stared at it, wide-eyed. "You're really real?"

"Sometimes." The unicorn lowered its head and touched Nicole's forehead with its horn. She slumped. "Ah, that's better. Now, let's see what's wrong with her."

Harm relaxed and cradled Nicole. He knew there'd been unicorns in the past, but they had vanished so long ago, no one in his generation had ever seen one, and he doubted even his grandparents had.

"I see." The unicorn looked at Harm. "A dragon broke her world. What a pity. It'll take a dragon to heal it. I won't be of much use here." It turned to go.

"Wait!" Harm reached out with one hand, surprised at how heavy it felt. "Can't you help her at all?"

The unicorn cocked its head. Although it didn't have much of a facial expression, it seemed to be smiling. "I put a damper on her suspicions and boosted her self-confidence. I also upped her trust in her own judgment and senses. That's all I could do. It is your job to make her understand the new world she woke up to."

"*My* job?" Harm's voice broke, but before he could ask more questions, the unicorn vanished, leaving behind nothing but a patch of greenery. "But what can *I* do?" Harm looked down at Nicole again. Although tears still ran over her face, she seemed to be sleeping peacefully. He so wanted to get up and carry her back to the parking lot, but with the strange fatigue and his broken leg … even though dragons healed in record times, his bones wouldn't mend instantaneously. What could he do? He pulled Nicole closer to keep her from sitting on the cold ground. It wouldn't have been a big discomfort for a dragon, but he knew how fragile human health was. It was definitely better to keep her from getting wet and cold. If only his arms would stop shaking.

He glanced at his watch. Colin would come to pick them up in about another half hour. He would have to contact him and let him know where they were.

Nicole's crying ceased, and her breathing became deeper. It didn't look as if she'd wake any time soon. His own eyelids drooped at the sight. He shook his head to clear it and used an opportunity he seldom got. He watched her face. Longingly, he registered every single freckle, the smoothness of her skin, and the length of her lashes. With guilty pleasure he imagined what it would be like to touch his lips to the sweet curve of her mouth.

Harm knew he was bonding but was completely defenseless. There was nothing he could do to stop himself from falling in love with Nicole. What would the Council do if they found out? Considering how much they hated Lydia's love for a human, it'd be a miracle if they'd let him live when they learned he was in love with a true witch. And a powerful one at that.

Fortunately that didn't matter. The chance that Nicole would ever return his feelings was close to nil. He lowered his head until it rested against her forehead. It was a very uncomfortable position, but he didn't care. This was his one chance to be as close to her as he'd ever wanted to be. And if it was the only time in his life his skin touched hers, he'd cherish it for the rest of his life. With flaring nostrils, he breathed in her scent of lilac and warmth and cleanliness. It was the most wonderful scent in the world and he committed every atom, every trace molecule of it to memory. He'd never, ever forget it, and he'd be able to call it up if—no, when—the Council had him exiled. It would make it easier to live on.

A ringing sound shocked him upright. Where did that … oh, right, his mobile. He rummaged around in his backpack and found it just as the ringing ended. He looked at the display. It was Colin's number. He called back immediately. When Colin answered on the first ring, he said, "Nicole's asleep. I'll tell you the full story when you're here. Can you pick us up on the forest road?"

"Is it the one leading uphill or the one that goes around the flat areas?"

It surprised Harm that Colin didn't ask why his sister slept, but he answered the question without hesitation. "The latter."

"I'll find you. Keep her warm." Colin ended the call.

"What do you think I'm doing?" Harm grumbled and pulled Nicole even closer.

It took Colin all of five minutes to arrive in a cloud of dust. "What happened?"

While Colin picked up his sister to put her in the passenger seat, Harm told him about the unicorn and pointed at the lush green that didn't show a sign of wilting. "She's an incredibly talented witch. The last unicorn sightings are more rumor than truth, it's been that long."

"But why is she sleeping then?" Colin fixed the seat-belt and adjusted Nicole's head so it would rest peacefully against the neck rest.

Harm explained about the unicorn's magic. "It should help her a bit. Maybe make it easier to cope with the fact that dragons and magic are real." He deliberately left out the part where the unicorn had said it was his job to look after the witch. It sounded too presumptuous.

"Hop on in." Colin helped him up and handed him the crutches. "We need to get her to bed as fast as possible. I don't want her to catch pneumonia this close to spring break."

Harm climbed into the back and pulled his crutches in, panting as if he'd run a marathon. Why was he so terribly tired?

"Can you drop me at home? With my broken leg I won't be any help getting her to bed, and I'm too tired to walk." It felt like defeat to admit that he wasn't up to another longish walk, but Harm was sure Colin wouldn't mind. Humans seemed a lot less competitive than dragons—*except when it comes to football,* he thought.

Naturally Colin agreed to take him home first. Half an hour later Harm unlocked the front door of his father's house. Why was it so hard to open it? With every day it seemed to be getting heavier. He longed to fly all the way back to their home in the mountains. It'd be quiet and peaceful there, and he could rest without having to worry about a maniacal dragon in a human body and a tongue-tied human in a dragon's hide, or about school. With a great yawn, he entered and then called out, "I'm home."

Silence greeted him, but that was nothing new. Mordekay didn't speak with him if he could help it, and Blackfeather had been monosyllabic even before he became a dragon. Harm hobbled into the living room, sat on the peach-colored sofa, and wondered why today's return felt different from all the others. He closed his eyes and listened. The silence was heavier than normal. He couldn't even make out his father's breathing, which was strange because in Smolinsky's body Blackfeather huffed and puffed like a steam engine. Also, the house smelled as if Mordekay had burnt their supper again. *I should go and look,* he thought, but he just couldn't get himself to move. He was so tired. *Only five minutes,* he thought before his thoughts drifted into dreamland. But even there, the scent of burnt meat wouldn't end. It permeated everything.

Nicole woke just as Colin left her room. "Colin?"

He peeked back in. "What is it, sis?"

She wondered that she was lying in her bed. Shouldn't she be in the woods? Hadn't Harm taken her on a … oh! The unicorn. She touched her head. Could she really still feel its horn there? Had that been real or another hallucination?

"Where's Harm?" The question seemed harmless enough. Maybe he could help her figure out what had happened.

"I took him home. He was too exhausted to walk."

Well, that had to be expected. After all, it wasn't exactly easy to walk with a broken leg. Still, Nicole had to fight a painful pull in her chest. If she really was going crazy, believing in magic and dragons and who knew what else, it would have been so much easier to confess it to Harm than to anyone else.

Colin entered her room again, closed the poster-covered door, and sat on her (for once book-free) bed. "What's bothering you, Nicci?"

The use of her childhood nickname brought tears to her eyes. She'd forgotten how close she and Colin used to be. Choking, she pressed the words out of her mind. "I'm going crazy."

She expected denial or an argument, but Colin just sat there waiting, so she continued. "Do you remember that strange incident in the woods a couple of months back? I thought I saw dragons. Real dragons! One was white, a smaller one was red, and then there was this huge, black monster. But the whole situation is completely muddled. I remember Smolinsky's face and Lydia's and Harm's and yours, but I can't for the life of me remember what happened. It's as if I'd been drugged."

She looked at Colin, feeling her desperation pour from every pore of her being.

"It's true. You were drugged." Colin stroked her cheek. "But when we tried to talk to you about it afterwards, you kept pushing us away."

"I'm a lunatic." For her, it seemed explanation enough.

"You're my sister, and Harm's and Lydia's friend." Colin put his hand on top of hers. "Don't push us out of your life."

"But don't you see? I'm getting more and more crazy. Today, I saw a unicorn, Colin." Tears ran over her face. "It was the most beautiful encounter I've had in my life, and I'm not even sure whether it was real or not. What if my mind is so addled that I'm no longer capable of living in the real world? I don't want to end up like grandma's sister."

Wordlessly Colin plucked something from her hair and held it out to her. It was a rather worn wood anemone, a flower that wouldn't bloom for a few more weeks. The tears in Nicole's eyes blurred her vision, but she took it very gently from his fingers. "It's been real?"

"Naturally." He smiled for the first time since he'd sat down.

"How come that you don't doubt?" Her fingers shook with the effort of holding the flower without smashing it accidentally. She'd seen a unicorn, for crying out loud. An honest-to-God unicorn. And if she believed Harm, she had been the one who called it. Searchingly she stared at Colin and lifted the flower towards him. "I'm holding this, and I still find it hard to believe. So how do you do it?"

Colin shrugged and stared at a Harry Potter picture at her wall, although she was sure he wasn't really seeing it. "It was easy for me," he said. "I'd rather be crazy together with Lydia than sane and without her."

A wave of longing washed over her, driving more and more tears from her eyes. Colin put his arms around her, and she leaned on his shoulder and let them flow freely.

Colin held his sister, glad she'd finally confided in him. He'd missed her company more than he'd cared to admit. It was a pity he couldn't do the same. If he burdened her with his problems right now, she might crack completely. He'd have to be strong and make sure she could heal.

His thoughts went to Lydia. What would she say when he told her about Nicole's breakdown? Would she consider it the breakthrough he was sure it was?

Oh Lydia. His heart contracted. *Why did you fall in love with me?* There was nothing that set him apart from other boys in his school, nothing that made him special. Nothing that justified her love for him.

And what if he proved to be a man just like any other human male he'd ever known or read about? Dragons bonded for life, humans normally not. What if he stopped loving her at some point? Tears seeped from the corners of his eyes. He would never forgive himself if he accidentally—or worse, deliberately—caused her pain. Like White Crow had been forced by circumstances to do to his wife.

His throat constricted at the thought. What if he turned out to be a cheating man like so many others? What if he got into a so-called midlife crisis someday and left Lydia? Wouldn't it break her heart? Would it break his?

The enormous fire of love in his heart scared him. What if so much love was more than he could handle? Holding his sister, his confusion, worry, and fears overwhelmed him, and he joined her crying because the one thing he was absolutely sure about and never questioned was the fact that right now he loved Lydia more than anyone he'd ever loved before.

Eighth Chapter

*H*arm jerked awake with every dragon sense screaming *danger*. The burnt scent had grown even stronger. Something in the house was most definitely wrong. Had Blackfeather gone out and left the oven running? But why didn't Mordekay turn it off. Was he trying to burn down the house? He'd better take care of it.

Reluctantly Harm got up and walked through the connecting door into the kitchen. The sight that met his eyes drove the last of his drowsiness from his mind. Blackfeather was lying on the floor. His dark suit had partially melted away and the skin of his body was bloody and raw. Most of his hair was gone, even his eyebrows and lashes, and he stared at the ceiling with unseeing eyes.

Dragon Bane. Harm crouched beside his father, secretly wondering why he was so calm. He fumbled for Blackfeather's jugular, and only realized he had been holding his breath when a deep sigh escaped his lips at the weak but regular pulse.

"Ouch." Pain nipped at his fingertips and he jerked them back. He stared at them. They looked raw too, so whoever had done this had used the Dragon Bane outwardly. Harm stood, hurried to the sink and washed his hands over and over until the tingling sensation stopped. Then he stepped out of the back door, frowning at the fact that it stood wide open. Where was Mordekay? If he had gone shopping groceries as ordered, he should be back any minute.

Harm grabbed the hose, turned on the water, returned inside and hosed Blackfeather down. It wasn't the gentlest way to get rid of the Dragon Bane, but it was the fastest. When he was sure that Blackfeather was free from the poison, he doused every part of the kitchen he could reach. It might cost them to get things repaired later, but he'd rather spend some of his hoard than touch any more Dragon Bane.

He began to pant after only a few minutes. Why did this exhaust him so much? That wasn't normal. He closed his eyes a moment and breathed deeply until he felt better. Then he continued to soak every available surface. When everything was drenched in water, he took the hose back outside, turned off the water and dropped the nuzzle where he stood. What next? He hurried back inside.

Blackfeather needed help, but whom could he ask? If he called an ambulance they'd take his father to a hospital for months. He'd seen it after Lydia's accident. And where would that leave him? He had to call Colin or Lydia or … yes, Angie was the person he needed. With flying fingers he dialed Angie's landline number, hoping she'd be at home.

Angie picked up at the third ring.

"Blackfeather's been attacked," he said without greeting. "Someone doused him with Dragon Bane."

"I'll be with you in a minute." Angie ended the call, and Harm crouched beside his father again. There was a hollow in his chest big enough to swallow the whole house. What if Blackfeather didn't make it? What if Angie didn't know what to do?

He forced himself to concentrate on the barely noticeable up and down of the man's chest. He listened to the bubbling noises from his mouth, and tried to ignore the stench of raw meat and fire. Who would do something like this? His heart felt as raw as his father looked.

When the front door clicked, he looked up, expecting Mordekay, but the dragon-turned-human remained missing. It was a rather disheveled Angie who entered. She hadn't even taken the time to put on a jacket.

"Let me see." She crouched beside him, bent over Blackfeather and examined him thoroughly. She even sniffed at him.

All the while, Harm hardly dared to breathe. Would she be able to help? Had he been right to hose Blackfeather down so harshly?

Finally, Angie sat up and smiled at Harm. "It wasn't Dragon Bane. His body is already mending, see?" She pointed to the eyelids that had been too disfigured to close over Blackfeather's eyes the last time Harm had looked. Now they looked rosy and covered the eyes as they should. Angie put her hand on Harm's shoulder. "It will take quite a while for him to recover from this, but he'll survive. And with his dragon's healing abilities there won't even be any scars."

A mountain seemed to lift from Harm's heart. His father would be alright. Not that it would change much between the two of them, but at least he still had a father. It was better than the alternative.

"What caused the burns if it wasn't Dragon Bane?" He was really curious about that. He'd always thought dragons were more or less impervious to everything except a knight's lance and Dragon Bane.

"It must have been some sort of acid. Hosing him down was the best thing you could have done." Angie got up and walked toward the hall. "My first aid kit is still in my car. If you've got sterile bandages and the like, you might want to fetch those. I don't think I've got enough for him."

For the next half hour, they worked mostly in companionable silence. They bandaged Blackfeather very gently and carried him upstairs where they put him to bed. He didn't wake, but he moaned a lot.

The injuries must be terribly painful. Harm bit his lip not to say something so obvious.

"Whoever did this," Angie said, "must have wanted your father to suffer but not to die."

Her words triggered a connection. Harm stared at her in disbelief. "Mordekay." He hastened to explain. "Mordekay isn't in the house. I thought he was out buying groceries because that's what I ordered him to do this morning, but he's not back yet, and normally Blackfeather would have accompanied him. We never let him go anywhere on his own."

"But weren't you using the Commanding Voice?" Angie frowned.

"Maybe he became immune. There are some known cases. Everything else fits. Mordekay is the only one who hates Blackfeather enough he'd love to see him dead, but he'd also never kill his own body." This idea sparked a whole array of connected thoughts. "If Mordekay is behind it, he must have had help. Blackfeather and I supervised him the whole time. He couldn't have bought acid without us noticing. I'm sure he used the chance to flee."

"It's extremely difficult to ignore the Commanding Voice." Angie scratched her chin. "Unless … May I use your phone?"

A little confused, Harm handed her his mobile.

"One of these days I'll need to get one of these after all." Angie dialed a number and waited a moment. "Ah, Colin. Do you have time to come over to Harm's for a minute? I need your nose."

She listened, said "Okay," ended the call, and handed the mobile back. "Now, let's see if Mordekay took anything."

To his surprise, Harm found it hard to leave Blackfeather. But there was nothing he could at the moment, so he followed Angie to the small room they'd given to Mordekay. The room was stripped of everything. Even the duvet was gone. Harm cursed.

"It's not your fault." Angie put her hand on his arm. "We should have known he's devious enough to break free. We should have presented him to the Council for his trial right after the incident in autumn instead of waiting for months to ferret out his supporters."

Harm ground his teeth, turned and walked back to Blackfeather's bedroom wordlessly. Somehow Mordekay had managed to get outside help. There must have been a loophole in one of the orders he'd given him. If only he'd been more specific with his commands. At the top of the stairs, he yawned. He grabbed the banister to fight a spell of dizziness.

At the same time the main door, still ajar from Angie's entry, slammed open and Colin raced up the stairs, eyes wide open with worry. "What happened? Are you all right?"

Harm shrugged, gathered his remaining strength, and stepped wordlessly through the bedroom door. He sat down beside

Blackfeather, leaving it to Angie, who escorted Colin into the room, to explain the situation.

"And what do you need me for?" Colin seemed less panicky but more angry now. Harm didn't care. Mordekay was on the run and it was his fault. He should have known. He should have expected something … anything … What if he tried to hurt Lydia again? Colin would never forgive him. Flogging himself for his carelessness, he nearly missed Angie's words.

"I want you to smell the supplies in the kitchen cupboards." Angie took Colin's arms and led him toward the door.

"Smell?" Colin's confusion was clearly visible, and it pulled Harm from his dark thoughts. Curious, he followed Angie and Colin back downstairs and into the water-filled kitchen.

Angie opened doors until she found the supplies in one of the hanging cupboards. Standing on a chair, she handed them down to Colin one by one. "Describe the smell," she said. "I'll explain the reason later."

"It's hard to describe smells." Colin looked worried. "Wouldn't it be easier if you told me what you're looking for and I confirmed or declined it?"

Angie shook her head. "I need an unbiased opinion. Just do your best."

So Colin did as she had asked. He smelled each item, described the scent as best he could, and put it on the table. They reached the teas last and Angie's hand shook a little as she picked up the first carton. Colin took the packet of Earl Grey tea and held it under his nose.

"It smells of lemons and sourness and … I don't know, maybe a hint of mint."

"Does it say anything about a flavor on the packet?" Angie asked. "Anything about lemon, lemon grass, orange, or mint?"

"No. It only says Earl Grey." Colin looked up to her. "Why is that so important?"

Angie climbed down from the chair and sat. "Someone, and I assume it was Mordekay with the help of his ally, put catnip into the tea." She looked at Harm, whose stomach had lurched at her words. *Catnip? Really?* Angie nodded as if to confirm his fears. "You drink quite a lot of tea, don't you?"

"I like strawberry fruit best." Harm nodded and yawned again, trying to hide it behind his hand. "But in the mornings Blackfeather and I drink Earl Grey. It's the best black tea ever invented by humans."

"And the best place to add the damned catnip." Angie balled her hands to fists.

"What's so bad about catnip?" Colin looked from Angie to Harm and back. "Is it poisonous for dragons?"

"No, but it makes us tired and reduces the potency of our magic." Harm sank onto another chair. "Now I finally know why I've been so very tired and lacking energy recently."

"With the power of the Commanding Voice diminished, it was easy for Mordekay to run." Angie got up, looking determined. "We need to inform the Council after all. We shouldn't have kept the information from them in the first place. After all, Mordekay is after Lydia's life. She has to leave for dragon lands immediately. I can't protect her all on my own."

Harm tried to tell her that she wasn't alone, not with him, Nicole, and Colin there, but his body finally claimed its need. Despite fighting the dizziness and leaden extremities, he slumped in his chair. A dark wave washed away his consciousness.

After helping Angie to put Harm to bed too, Colin sat on the sofa and mulled over the situation. Fierce pain squeezed his heart. It wouldn't be easy to convince Lydia to move back to the dragons' village with still four weeks to go until spring break. But it was imperative she go. Angie wouldn't be able to protect her on her own, and he was more a liability than help, now that Mordekay knew Lydia had truly bonded with him. But how could he convince Lydia?

Angie entered and sighed. "They're both asleep. Harm is doing fine, but Blackfeather is not healing well."

Colin forced his thoughts away from Lydia and concentrated at the problem at hand. "Blackfeather has had problems accessing his dragon side right from the start. If only there was a way to turn him back into his old self."

"Ignoring that right now Mordekay is still in it, he'd die in his current state." She sat down beside him. "We'll have to think about something else. Also, we'll have to find a way to make Lydia understand how important it is to leave the humans for now."

"I've been thinking about that." Colin stared at his hands. "Lydia is so fascinated by all things human that she's planning on staying a human for good. She decided that she really wants to get better in school, so she can get a job later."

"That's not possible." Angie frowned. "It'll be hard to make her realize that."

"I know." Colin's throat was dry as sandpaper, scratching the words as he spoke. "But her ambition might be a way to get her to leave."

"How so?" Angie turned sideways, pulling one leg up onto the sofa and hugging it with both arms.

"There's this boy, Luke Gentry. Harm introduced me to him. He's a straight-A student in my school year." Colin couldn't help but worry his lip. "I already talked to him and, provided you agree, he'd be willing to become Lydia's tutor."

"The Council will never allow another human to come."

"That's not what I meant." Colin looked at her. His worry for Lydia clouded every other thought. "If we promise her that Luke will tutor her after her return, we might get her to agree more easily. She's determined to learn everything about humans."

Angie smiled at him, and it warmed him nearly as much as Lydia's smiles did. "That isn't a half bad idea, Colin." She got up. "I'll go and talk to Lydia. She needs to know what has happened anyway. Also, she might be the only one around who can help Blackfeather, if she puts her mind to it. Will you stay with Harm and Blackfeather a little?"

"Sure." Colin watched her leave and then returned to his bleak thoughts.

"A penny for your thoughts."

Colin's eyelids flew open and he looked up. Harm had somehow managed to come downstairs on his own despite his crutches. "I ... I'm sorry. I didn't mean to fall asleep."

Harm turned his rear to the sofa, bent his one functioning knee, and let himself fall backward when he couldn't hold his weight any longer. "Oof. I fear you'll have to help me get up again later."

"No problem." Colin watched Harm from the side. His friend looked better. The dark shadows under his eyes were much less pronounced, and there was verve in his gaze again. How long would it take his body to get rid of the catnip?

"How's my ... how's Blackfeather? Will he fully recover?"

Colin scratched his chin. Should he tell him the truth? Of course; anything else would be foolish. "Angie doesn't know yet. With the problems he's had accessing his dragon magic, he might not make it."

Harm pressed his lips together; surely an unconscious gesture.

"He's your father. It's completely natural that you're worried about him."

"I'm not … I mean, he's not…" Harm's mouth snapped shut.

Colin put his hand on Harm's arm. "If you don't talk, I can't help you. You are partially human, and humans do need to talk to cope with their emotions. I bet you do too."

Harm nodded, but his eyes remained wary as he spoke. "It's all my fault. If I had come home earlier…" His voice trailed off.

"… Mordekay would have done it some other time." Colin tried to be as reassuring as he could. He needed Harm to protect Lydia, and for that the young dragon needed a clear head. "It was his plan, after all. He knew you'd have to go to school and meet friends and the like."

Harm shook his head. "If I hadn't helped Mordekay in the first place, we wouldn't be in this mess."

"And you still wouldn't know how much Blackfeather loves you."

"Does he?" Harm stared directly into Colin's eyes. "He never shows me affection. He never praises me. Not that I'd been used to that. Mordekay never did that either. But I'd thought a different father would treat me differently."

Colin wracked his brain for the best answer. "All your life, Blackfeather pretended you were nothing but the son of an owner he hated. Do you think it is easy to change a habit of seventeen or eighteen years?"

A glimmer of hope appeared on Harm's face. "You think he likes me after all?"

"He wouldn't have done what he did if it hadn't been for you," Colin said with finality. "He expected his body to die and accepted it so he could save you."

"And Lydia."

"And Nicole." Colin nodded.

"And you." Harm looked at his hands. "Do you think he'll ever be able to admit that?"

"Maybe you should talk to him. Talking is the humans' secret weapon after all." Colin smiled and watched Harm stare at his hands, lost in thought. Hopefully he had helped him at least a little and not given him false hope. Blackfeather could have had other reasons to do what he did.

Harm looked up at him. "You know, you're right. I need to talk to Father." Tears glittered in his eyes, something Colin had not yet seen. He hadn't even known dragons could cry aside from the crystal tears they cried when they lost their true love.

Harm blinked a couple of times. "I think I'll sit at his side for a while. Maybe he'll wake."

Colin helped him up and watched him climb the stairs by hopping up one step at a time. The determination on Harm's face made him proud but also worried him. "Please," he whispered to no one in particular, "let me be right. Harm needs a good father more than anything else."

Ninth Chapter

On the ride to Harm's house, I sat silently beside Angie to let her feel my anger about the planned departure. I didn't want to leave. Not yet. We'd agreed on spring break, which was still weeks away. What difference did it make that Mordekay had fled? He was a human now and had no access to magic. He couldn't harm me or anyone I liked without hurting himself. I frowned some more, but Angie simply ignored it.

"This is a great opportunity for you to learn something new," she said without taking her gaze from the road. It had gone dark a while back, and she had to concentrate. Still she found the time to lecture me. "And healing magic is terribly important. Only very few dragons have the ability to use it, but as a queen-in-the-making your power should be big enough."

I wasn't so sure about that. Still, Blackfeather had saved my life, so I owed him a try at least. I gazed at the road. Despite the streetlamps it was hard to see, as if it didn't want to be used. But maybe that was just my imagination.

"Trust your parents." Angie threw me a sideways smile and looked back at the road. "They'll help if you let them."

As if I knew how to contact them. So far it'd always been them contacting me from that white nothingness they seemed to live in. I pressed my lips together as she pulled into the driveway. Sure I'd do my best, but I didn't expect it to amount to much.

"Why can't I simply order him to get well?" After all, the Commanding Voice was one of the spells that seemed to come to me naturally.

"It only works on the conscious parts of your mind, and those do not affect healing. You'll need to convince his subconscious that he needs to live." Naturally Angie had an answer to that question. I should have known. Pouting, I followed her inside and up the stairs.

Blackfeather's bedroom was right at the top. When my gaze fell on the oozing wounds in his face and his bloody hands on a forest green cover with dark yellow leaves, my stomach turned. Hurriedly I focused on the surprisingly feminine room. The wallpaper sprouted tiny roses, the curtains were of a dark, wine red velvet contrasting nicely with the white furniture. Unfortunately, they also reminded me of the blood. Again I turned a little and stared unbelievingly at a dressing table with a gold framed mirror. I understood that Mordekay wouldn't bother changing the room's decoration, but why hadn't Blackfeather done anything about this? Had he been so preoccupied with protecting his son? Again my mind called up his wounds, and this time I wasn't able to push the picture away. But I didn't want to see them. There was nothing I could do about them. I just knew it. Regardless of what Angie said, I was a failure at magic.

My parents' soothing warmth enveloped me like an embrace, and I finally dared to look in the direction of the queen-sized bed again. Standing right in the middle of the room with only the head touching a wall, it dominated everything. The dark green cover suited Blackfeather much better than the rest of the room.

Harm was sitting on a metal kitchen chair beside the bed, and Colin was just setting down a tray with tea and biscuits at its end.

"We haven't had dinner yet," he said apologetically and offered me a cookie. With my stomach still revolting, I declined and walked over to Angie. Blackfeather's head rested on the pillow. What little remained of the skin was as pale as a sheet of paper, and he breathed laboriously. I'd never seen him so unresponsive before.

"Why isn't he waking up?" I stepped closer and took Angie's hand, only for reassurance. Still I had to fight nausea whenever my gaze fell on Blackfeather's face.

"He's unconscious because his injuries are healing way too slowly. You'll need to help him connect with the magic in his body or he won't survive the night."

Harm emitted a moan that reminded me of an injured dog. I glanced at him. He was just as pale as the still existing parts of skin of his father. I bit my lips. Harm's pain cut into my heart like a knife. If only I could help Blackfeather. But despite Angie's conviction that I should be able to do something, my innards told me I'd be of no use. But I'd promised to try. "What will I have to do?"

Angie explained in great detail. "And once you're inside his defenses, you just have to find his true self and tell it to heal. That part should be pretty easy."

"I understand," I said. "Getting to his subconscious is the hard part, right?"

"Are you game?" Her green eyes bored into mine as if she was willing me to help, but I'd already made up my mind when

Harm had moaned. I would do whatever I could to help him and his father.

She made me lie down on a wine red rug beside the bed. I closed my eyes and breathed the way she had told me to. One, two, three—in—one, two, three, four—out; over and over again. After a while a very strange sensation tingled through my body. It was as if I was being pulled in two but there was no pain. Floating near the ceiling, I stared at my body in its human form below. Angie was holding my hand. It took me a moment to realize that my floating self was in its dragon form, just a lot smaller. I was surrounded by the warm light of my parents' presence but couldn't see them anywhere. But even so, I felt less anxious—until I turned as instructed and looked at Blackfeather's defenses.

A huge black dragon hung in a dark cloud over the injured body. Its eyes glowed with the dull red of burning coals, and the black steam drifting from its nostrils fueled the clouds. It looked like a nightmare version of Mordekay's dragon form. I mean, Mordekay himself was a nightmare, but this version looked the part. No wonder Blackfeather had so many problems accessing his magic.

I flew down and out of sight of the black dragon like Angie had told me to do. She said that there'd be a blind spot somewhere and that I had to find it, but she hadn't been able to tell me how said blind spot would look in this semi-real world.

So I circled the dragon and studied him for a while. Nothing presented itself, and that meant I had to tease him with pseudo-attacks. My mouth went dry. How could I, at the size of a Golden Retriever, survive an encounter with a dragon at least ten times my size, even if this wasn't the real world?

I didn't really want to, but the memory of that strangled sound Harm had made drove me forward. I charged at him at the highest speed I could muster, swerving at the last moment.

The black dragon reacted, but he was very sluggish. I attacked again, spitting fire at the black clouds. That seemed to help a little. The dark vapor thinned, revealing a light glow between the black dragon's claws. Maybe that was the blind spot I'd been looking for. So I targeted it with my third attack. The black dragon's left paw rose, as sluggish as before, and I recognized the leather skin of the entrance to a typical tepee. So, instead of swerving away from the paw, I sped up toward it.

Pain scorched my back as the black dragon's claws ripped through the flying membrane of my wings. I howled, curling up into a ball mid-flight. *I can't do this. I need to wake up.* But before the words were even half thought, I cannoned through the tepee entrance into a completely different place.

Everything around me was of the same luminous white. I wasn't entirely clear about up and down. It resembled floating though a cloud, only everything was far more uniform. To my surprise, the pain in my back had stopped the second I'd entered. So I floated through the white nothingness looking for Blackfeather. I found him curled into a tight, gray ball with his hands over his head and ears. He resembled a rolled-up woodlouse. I nudged him, but he didn't unroll.

"Open," I ordered with my Commanding Voice, but he didn't even stir. Hadn't Angie said that once I was through his defenses, things would be easy? How could I order someone around who refused to hear? I nudged him again. He was cold like a stone.

My mind raced. Was it possible that through all the years of hiding from Mordekay's prying he'd turned himself, his true center, into a ball of stone? Was this gray ball a symbol for his calcified emotions? If so, how could I get him to open at least a little?

Something warm and soothing rose in my throat. A song—and judging by the warmth, one my parents had sent—erupted into this white world. It was only a melody, rising slowly up and down and up again like a brook bubbling over stones.

The whiteness changed. Vague shapes appeared. A tepee here, a bubbling brook there, an open fire with a pot of stew between them. The outlines of trees and mountains appeared in the distance like faded memories. And the gray ball stirred. Very slowly the arms sank down and Blackfeather's face became visible. He didn't uncurl, but he looked at me.

"You will need to rediscover your feelings, you know," I told him as loud and clear as I could. "No one can live without them."

"Yes, Your Majesty." He uncurled and stood up, looking around in bewilderment.

Only then did I realize that I was still using my Commanding Voice. Oops! Well, it couldn't be helped. "And while you're at it, heal your body," I ordered him.

"Naturally." He bowed stiffly and vanished together with the faded-looking scenery.

I blinked and opened my eyes. Flowery walls and white furniture greeted me. I'd done it. I sat up hurriedly and looked over to the bed despite the dizziness that threatened to pull me down again. My back hurt as if someone had ripped off my wings. I frowned.

Angie's hand eased me back down. There was a worried frown on her face. "Take it easy. Healing takes a lot of energy."

"It didn't feel like healing someone, you know?" I struggled against her hand to sit up again. Blackfeather should be healing and I wanted to see it, but her hold on my shoulder was too strong, and the pain in my back spread from my shoulder blades downward. So in the end, I relaxed.

"Tell me what happened." Angie bent over me and stared into my eyes.

My mouth opened to obey, when I realized that she'd been trying to compel me with her voice. Hey now, that wouldn't do. She couldn't just go around putting spells on her foster daughter now, could she? On the other hand, it wasn't a secret or anything and she did seem terribly worried, so I condescended. I told her everything I'd discovered in the white world, but when she asked me about before, I found that I couldn't remember. There were fragments of something black, or gray vapor and of fire and pain, but I couldn't recall anything else. What the …?

"That shouldn't have happened," Angie said. "Usually everyone can recall the entry. When you're in the village, get Cassandra to look at you. She's the best healer there is. If there's something to be found, she will find it. And now let's have a look at Blackfeather."

She helped me to my feet. I swayed. Immediately Colin offered me another kitchen chair. I sat down with relief. My back was still killing me. I must have twisted it when I was lying on the floor. When I glanced at the window, I noted that the moon had already risen. Dear me, how long had I been out?

My gaze returned to Blackfeather. His skin was still very pale, but at least the wounds that had been oozing transparent liquid before had closed. A thin, pink layer of new skin covered most of them. We watched him silently, expectantly.

After a while, his eyelids fluttered, and soon after he opened his eyes. His gaze fell on Harm, and a slow smile spread over his face. "You're safe!" He closed his eyes again and breathed for a while before he opened them once more and looked the room over. When he noticed Angie, he said, "Mordekay … He used sulfuric acid on me … He hates Harm … You must protect him."

"I will." Standing on my side of the bed, Angie took his right hand. "He'll be going to the village with Lydia tonight."

"Good." Blackfeather's eyelids drooped again, but he only blinked a few times and turned to Harm. "Mordekay said … he'll kill us as soon as … he gets his body back … I tried to pull up the dragon defenses. Really, I did." He grabbed Harm's hand with his and tried to get up. His breathing became strained.

"I promise I'll always be alert." Harm pushed him down very, very gently. With a sigh, Blackfeather sank back into his cushions. Soon after he fell asleep again. When his breathing was peaceful and even, Angie decided it would be a good time for everyone to go packing. We left Harm at his father's side and walked downstairs, out of the house. After a quick hug and kiss, Colin got into his car to drive back to his place.

A ball of disappointment and ice formed in my stomach. Didn't Colin like me anymore?

But then he rolled down his window and waved. "I'll pick you up in half an hour, if possible, with Nicole."

Tenth Chapter

Half an hour later, I finished packing. There was no use in taking along too much stuff. First, I surely had plenty at my parents' house and second, Angie had reminded me that dragons did have a weight limit if we wanted to maneuver properly while flying. My stomach contracted when I thought about leaving everything behind that I knew and loved. Why did I have to be born a princess?

Colin and Nicole entered my room. Immediately, Nicole threw her arms around me. "I've been such an idiot."

Surprised and confused, I returned the hug. Before I could ask for Nicole's reasons, my friend pulled me down on my bed.

"You know, with all the books I'd been reading and my mother always telling me I couldn't tell the difference between reality and dream, I thought … I mean, after that incident, I thought … I've been so stupid and silly and extremely unfair to you. You and Harm are my friends. I shouldn't have cut you out of my life for so long."

"So you're accepting now that we're…?" I didn't dare use the word 'dragons,' so I let my voice ebb away.

"I don't know what I believe yet." Nicole stared at her hands. "Fact is, I tried a spell and it did work. Maybe there really is more to this world than Mom knows. Colin is accepting it without question, so maybe I'm not going crazy after all. I'm prepared to see how things turn out."

"I'm glad you are." I hugged Nicole, acutely aware of the tiny flames dancing in my heart. Her change of mind made me happier than I'd ever expected. I hadn't even known how much I'd missed her. "How about a hot chocolate?"

"I'm game," Colin said from the door. He let his sister pass and grabbed both of my hands to pull me closer. When his lips met mine, my body tingled from the tips of my hairs to the soles of my feet. I felt warm and protected. For a moment, everything faded but the sensation of his closeness. I sucked in his scent, loving him more with every breath. How could I be so happy? My mind already showed me pictures of a clutch of eggs in a softly padded nest. I jerked back. *Not yet!* Not as long as Mordekay was still around, and anyway, I wanted to become a real human before I committed to a family.

"What's wrong? Did I hurt you?" Colin gazed into my eyes with a worry frown on his forehead, and my knees trembled once more. How did he do that?

"No…nothing. I just want my chocolate." I blushed, grabbed his hand and pulled him downstairs where I'd heard the clinks of metal on porcelain. Angie was already preparing my favorite drink. Right now I was grateful for the dragons' acute hearing.

Colin sat on a kitchen chair, pulling me down on his lap, while Nicole took the mugs from Angie and placed them on the table.

"I can take you to the clearing whenever you're ready." Angie sat down opposite of Colin and me.

"Aren't you coming too?" My eyes widened, and I grabbed my mug to hide my confusion.

"I need to look after Blackfeather, and I have to trace Mordekay." She didn't look at me. "There's no one else who can."

"And you've also got to convince our parents to let us go and visit Lydia's home village," Colin said.

Nicole paled. "I'm not sure if I'm ready yet."

"Well, it will be a few more days before Mom and Dad will yield." Colin grinned. "You know how strict they are when it comes to missing school, and Angie refuses to use magic on them."

"It turns humans into slaves with nothing they can do against it." Angie's face was stern. "You only need to look at Blackfeather's problems to understand why I don't use magic on friends or their families. Especially not the Commanding Voice."

For a moment, no one spoke. Then Colin cleared his throat and said to her, "Apropos Blackfeather. I think you should talk to Harm. There's something going on inside of him that he won't tell me. Whenever I hint at it, he blocks. Maybe he'll confide in you."

"I noticed. I'll get him to help me with the search and see if I can pry something out of him." Angie winked at me, which lit up my mood considerably. "Now, Nicole, are you going to watch Lydia change? It might be good for you."

Nicole's jaw moved up and down as if she wanted to say something but couldn't. I remembered my fears when it had been time for me to recall the accident and how I had cringed inwardly. So I reached out, put my hand on her arm, and tried to look sympathetic. "You don't have to if you're not ready yet. No one will force you."

"It's complicated." She breathed deeply, closed her eyes, and sipped her cocoa. "On one hand I really want to watch. I've always dreamed of meeting a dragon or a unicorn. On the other hand there's this huge lump in my throat when I only think about it. I'm so scared that I'm making all this up, that I'm as crazy as my grandma was."

I looked at Colin with raised eyebrows.

"Long story," he whispered. "I'll tell you some other time."

I turned back to Nicole, doing my best to send loving understanding towards her. "You know, as long as you don't talk about dragons and unicorns and magic with someone who will think you're crazy, you won't run into problems. I mean, if you're truly crazy, so are Harm and Colin and Angie and I. And in that case talking to us wouldn't get you into trouble, right?"

Her face lit up and she stopped staring at her mug. "That's true. Okay, I'll come along."

"I can't stay around for the change," Angie said. "I promised Harm I'd be back in half an hour. That's just enough time to drop you off at the parking lot near the forest."

"That's okay. I can pick Nicole up when Lydia's gone." He looked at Nicole. "Have you got your mobile?"

She nodded. As soon as we'd finished our drinks, Nicole, Angie and I set out for the forest. In the parking lot, I hugged Angie.

"Someone from the Council should be waiting in the clearing," she said. "They agreed to come and pick you up."

It still bothered me that dragons were using mobiles and landlines, but in this case it really had been useful. How else would Angie have been able to arrange my escape? I hugged her some more, shouldered my pack and followed Nicole, who was already waiting on the path to the clearing.

Silently we hiked up the hill. When we neared our final destination, Nicole said, "I'm scared."

"I won't hurt you, I promise."

"I know. It's not that." She looked up at the overcast sky. "I'm scared that it might be true that you're a dragon, and at the same time scared that it might not be true." Her smile wavered. "I think that's one of the reasons I tried to stay away. All these emotions are so confusing."

That was something I knew all too well. I patted her shoulder. Just a few minutes later, we emerged in the clearing. It looked just like it had before. At some point during winter Angie must have been back to clear away Mordekay's utensils and the broken trees.

"Close to the trees is the best place for watchers." I walk toward the flat rock near the center of the clearing, clearly remembering the time I had watched Harm change and how shocked I had been. "You might want to sit down, just in case the change alarms you too much."

I turned and saw that Nicole had followed my advice. So I lifted my arms toward the sky. It didn't matter that I couldn't see the sun or the moon, I felt the light prickle on my skin. With a mental shove, I pushed my clothes and the traveling bag into the compartment dragons had used for this kind of thing ever since they became shifters, and allowed my form to take on its natural body. It felt so good to return to myself I purred like a kitten. If only Colin could be a dragon too, but the ritual Mordekay had used was too dangerous and also it would need the sacrifice of a dragon. I sighed as my wings started to unfold. Well, if Colin couldn't become a dragon, I had to become a human. My mind was just contemplating the tutor Angie had hired—hopefully he'd be nice—when Nicole screamed. I opened my eyes.

A dark shadow galloped toward me with something long and pointy sticking out of it. Just at that moment, the clouds opened and a lonely sunbeam lit up the metal of a knight on a horse and the barbs on the tip of his lance.

Nicole's scream echoed through the clearing when the white dragon exploded into the air leaving a whirl of sand and small pellets in its wake. The tip of the knight's lance missed Lydia by inches. Where on earth had the knight come from? How had he known they'd be here?

Nicole scrambled to her feet, ready to flee. But Lydia didn't fly away as she'd expected. She hovered just out of the knight's reach. Was she looking for her?

"Fly away," she called. Unfortunately that got the attention of the knight. He turned his horse and galloped toward her. Her heart jumped into her throat. Instead of running for cover, she stood frozen, staring at the tip of the lance.

The dragon shot a stream of fire, but aimed it at the rocky ground so it wouldn't spread. It was still enough to scare the horse. It reared. The knight crashed to the ground, and the horse raced off, followed by choice curses from the knight. Nicole thought his voice, although muffled by the helmet, sounded quite young. *I should flee,* shot through her mind. *Now, before he recovers.* She had barely lifted her foot when the knight was back on his feet, ran toward her and grabbed her arm. Boy, was he fast. Nicole did her best to free her arm, but the knight unsheathed his sword and held the tip toward her belly. She froze again.

"Come down, or I'll kill her." The knight's voice wasn't loud, but obviously enough for Lydia to hear. She swooped down, claws outstretched. The knight shoved Nicole aside and attacked the dragon with a yell. Lydia landed a few steps from them and reached for Nicole in vain.

Nicole stumbled, trying to keep her balance, but it was impossible. She crashed to the ground just as a group of young men broke from the trees on the other side of the clearing, screaming at the tops of their lungs, brandishing clubs and baseball bats.

Soft paws with unyielding claws closed around Nicole, and for a second, panic coursed through her. Then she realized that Lydia had grabbed her and was pushing her up toward her back, but her relief was short-lived.

Lydia fought hard to evade the knight's sword and that made climbing onto her back nearly impossible. Also, the young men had arrived and made it too hard for Lydia to lift off.

Nicole clung to the short spikes on Lydia's back with all her might and pulled herself up. Wasn't there a spell she could use in a situation like this? But the only one she remembered was the one she'd used at Harm's urging. Calling a unicorn surely wouldn't help. She found a place between the wings where she settled just as Lydia reared, screaming with pain.

At the same time, the knight staggered and fell. Blood welled from a rip in his leg where Lydia's claw had pierced the armor. A moan escaped his lips. The young men doubled their efforts to keep Lydia from flying away. Nicole had had about enough. If there wasn't a spell, she'd make one up and to hell with the consequences. Closing her eyes, she tried to remember the feeling she'd had when she'd called the unicorn. Instantly, the tips of her fingers started to tingle.

"Ene mene mox, mice rattle in the box. Ene mene may, and you'll fly away." She pointed at the young men and allowed the magic to shoot out of her fingertips. Instantly, blackness claimed her.

Pain raced through my side where the knight's sword had pierced my thick skin, but he was down on the ground too, so that was a plus. It meant only the youngsters with their clubs remained. Sure, it hurt whenever they hit me, but a dragon's body was a lot tougher than a human's. Surely I could outlast them until the Council member showed up who'd been meant to pick me up.

On my back, Nicole chanted a nonsense rhyme, and a heatwave shot past my ear, narrowly missing it, and slammed into the group of youngsters. They flew halfway across the clearing as if a giant fist had boxed them out of the way.

I took the chance and lifted off the ground. Nicole wobbled, which meant she was probably unconscious, but that was something I couldn't consider right now. I strained my wings harder than ever before, but flew so much slower with the added weight. Gaining height felt like racing uphill. Hopefully I hadn't reached my weight limit yet. It just wouldn't do if I crashed while carrying Nicole. If only I could make it into the clouds, I'd be able to use one of the air currents to carry her.

My wing muscles complained louder with every beat. I was more tired than ever before, but I had to make it. With sheer determination I dove into the clouds and used the first current I found to keep aloft. Nicole was still not moving on my back. What would I do if she slipped off? I knew I wouldn't be able to catch her in time. *Where to?* I asked myself. *I have to find help for*

Nicole. But I couldn't land in Harm's or Angie's garden without being seen by humans.

"White Crow!" My voice sounded thin this high up, but I was glad I'd thought of my childhood protector. Since my wings had recovered a little, I headed toward the mountains. White Crow would know what to do. He always knew. And together we would be able to figure out where the knight had come from and how he had known I'd be in the clearing at that time. For clearly the attack had been deliberate. The sword and armor had been as real as my scales, not the fake stuff re-enactment people wore. The other attackers had looked far more like a bunch of youngsters called from the streets to help out. There'd been no discipline to their attack, and their gazes had been dull, as if they weren't masters of their own decisions. Could the knight have been a dragon in league with Mordekay? But which dragon in his right mind would dress up as a knight of all things, and who would help a lunatic like Mordekay?

I remembered the law that no dragon was better or worse than any other dragon until his own actions doomed him. And Mordekay had certainly doomed himself. *But most dragons don't know that yet,* I thought. *So maybe he did convince someone with lies and deceit to help him. I need to phone Angie as soon as I set down.*

I scanned the mountain range below me for a good landing place. Finally I set down in the same clearing I'd used with Harm the first time. Since Nicole was still unconscious, and too heavy for me to carry, I remained in my dragon form. It was a little difficult to maneuver between the trees, but I reached the house without losing Nicole.

White Crow stood in front of the door with his arms folded over his chest. "What happened?" He didn't seem surprised to see me here.

A wave of relief flooded through me, and I turned into my human form. I told him about the attack and how Nicole had saved us.

"Which spell did she use?" He caught Nicole and I was glad for it. It would have been awkward to turn during the transformation to catch someone from my back.

"I think she made one up. It sounded like a self-made nursery rhyme." Back in human form, I swayed. Blood was running down my side. The knight must have gotten through my hide somewhere. Combined with the flight, I felt as if I hadn't slept in years, which was probably due to a loss of blood.

White Crow nodded and carried Nicole into the house. I followed him, feeling like a visitor even though it belonged to me now that my parents were dead. When Nicole was resting on the sofa, White Crow examined my wound.

"You were lucky. It's only a shallow cut. A little higher and he'd have cut an artery." He fetched a Band Aid and an orange fluid in a plastic bottle that he applied it to my wound. I bit my lip because it stung. He covered the cut with a generously-sized Band Aid. "It'll heal by tomorrow. Come."

He led me into the kitchen and began to prepare a meal; a big one.

"Are you trying to feed an army?" My eyes went wide as I took in the amount of food he piled on the table.

"Eat something. You need to regain your strength." He pushed a plate with fruit and bread toward me. "I'll explain as soon as Nicole comes to. I don't like to repeat myself."

I pouted. Why couldn't he tell me now? But obedient like a fledgling I bit into a slice of bread.

Even after I'd eaten, we had enough time to cook a clear broth and spaghetti bolognese before Nicole stirred. When she tried to sit up, she seemed so frail, I hovered beside her to make sure she didn't fall off the sofa.

"Where am I?" Nicole gazed around, taking in the peach-colored walls, the dark wooden floorboards, the pine wood furniture, and the lack of decorations in the room, before she looked at me. "What happened to the knight?"

"Eat first." White Crow handed her the bowl with broth and she obeyed. I sat beside her on the sofa and told her the part of the tale she hadn't followed, suddenly understanding White Crow's dislike of repetitions. When I was finished I watched her eat nearly everything White Crow and I had prepared. Only one muffin remained uneaten in the end. I stared at her in awe. I couldn't have eaten half of it, not even in my dragon form.

"I'm sure you wonder why you've been so hungry." White Crow had always been someone to get right to the point. "I know Lydia is curious." I blushed and he winked at me.

Nicole didn't notice. Her gaze was glued to White Crow's face as if she found him familiar.

"Lydia told me you made up a spell to help her during the fight. Is that right?"

Nicole nodded.

"That is the reason why you were so extremely hungry and why you fainted." White Crow sat on a comfy chair beside the sofa and settled in for a longish explanation. "A spell needs energy and can draw it from many sources. The easiest are the energy reserves of the caster. That's what you used instinctively and therefore your hunger was enormous. More advanced magic users, at least in dragon society, pull their magic from the sun. It's the biggest energy source there is. And a few are capable of pulling energy from their enemies, weakening them in the process."

"Does that mean magic users always have to eat this much if they can't use the sun?" Nicole's eyes widened with a hint of panic. "What will my parents think if this happens more often?"

White Crow shrugged. "I've read that some truly rare magic users were able to draw energy from Earth, but haven't found the slightest hint at how they did that. So all I can teach you is how to use the sun."

"Are you a magic user too?" Nicole's eyes grew even wider. If she wasn't careful they'd pop out of her face.

"No, but I've always been reading a lot, and dragons are natural magic users, so their library is full of all things relating to magic." He smiled at her. "What do you say, are you interested in learning the basics?"

I saw the longing in Nicole's eyes but also a hint of panic. Before she could decline the offer, I said, "Naturally she'd like to learn, but can you keep it a secret?"

"Yes, please." Nicole wrung her hands. "I don't want anyone to know about this, especially not my brother."

"That should not be a problem." White Crow got up. The front door clicked open, and my head snapped around. White Crow obviously had noticed too because he changed the subject immediately. "I'll prepare a bed for you."

He vanished through a second door in the back of the living room that I hadn't noticed before because it was covered in the same wallpaper as the walls. I understood. He didn't want anyone to know he was still alive, and this could only be a welcome visitor since my parents' and my magic would prevent anyone else from entering the house.

"Would you like to share a room with me?" I asked Nicole before she could ask a question. I winked at her and nodded to the door to the living room that just opened. She seemed to understand because she nodded lightly.

Two white-clad dragons in their human forms walked in. The older one said, "I am sorry, but Her Majesty will not remain here. She is needed in the palace."

"I've got a palace?" My heart sank as I envisioned a Disney-style castle in pink and light blue with sparkling gold inlays and rainbow buntings and flags. What a nightmare.

"Of sorts." The younger dragon-man grinned. He reminded me a little of Harm, but by the look of him, he was the older one's son.

"What about Nicole?" Despite the young dragon's friendly smile, my stomach was in free fall.

"The human may stay here if you wish. We will provide a servant, but she is not entitled to visit the castle without a supervising dragon." The older man folded his arms in front of his chest, indicating that he wouldn't discuss the point. I snorted. What was I if not a supervising dragon?

Before my anger flared up, Nicole put her hand on my arm. "Maybe you'll like it there. And I'm better off here. It's surely less stiff and formal."

I turned and looked at her, and she jerked her head *imperceptibly* at the rest of the house. I understood. She wanted to stay so she could learn with White Crow, and my presence would hinder more than help. I sighed, forcing my stomach back to where it belonged, hugged her and turned to the two unknown dragons. "In that case, let's go."

Eleventh Chapter

Harm stared at the sunken face of his father, his heart full of worry. Would he live? What would he do if Blackfeather died? Not many in the dragon community would take him in. And the Council would surely forbid Lydia to keep close contact. It wouldn't do to have the future queen associate with the son of a traitor, even if he wasn't Mordekay's real son. It was hard to admit that these worries paled against the possibility of losing yet another father. For a moment he wished he could have a normal father, like Nicole and Colin, but then he realized that what he truly wanted was to be acknowledged by Blackfeather. The last few months they'd lived in the same house, side by side, and it had felt as if he was on his own. He'd talked more to Mordekay than to his father. Did Blackfeather hate him? Did he consider him responsible for his change?

His thoughts returned to the problem he'd been mulling on for so long. Why had Blackfeather really taken over Mordekay's body? Had it been so he could be a dragon? That didn't seem likely considering how little effort he put into learning their magic. Had he wanted to save Lydia so the dragons would have a queen? That didn't make sense either. After all, Blackfeather had been a slave and was bound to hate dragons that used slaves, so why would he fight for a queen who for all he knew might approve of slavery? The only reason that did make sense was that he sacrificed himself to save his son. If that were true, it was an incredible display of love. But why then had he shown so little of it in the last few months when they'd lived together? Harm had done his best to get at least a tiny little bit of praise, a smile, or just a pat on the shoulder, but nothing had been forthcoming whatsoever. *He doesn't really like me*, Harm thought, and considering how long he'd been Mordekay's son, it didn't surprise him.

He worried his lower lip thinking of the times before they had moved here. He'd felt inadequate most of the time, but not unloved. His grandmother had showered him with affection as long as she'd lived, and some of the neighboring fledglings had been his friends. Shortly before Mordekay uprooted him, a girl even had admitted she liked him. He blushed at the memory.

"Nice thoughts?" Blackfeather's voice was hoarse. Hurriedly Harm fetched the mug with water he'd prepared and helped his father drink.

"Thank you," Blackfeather said and looked at him in silence for a while. Then he breathed deeply. "I need to apologize."

"What for?"

"I don't remember who, but someone ordered me to speak to you, and I know it is the right thing to do. I just don't know if I'll find the words." Blackfeather's gaze went to the ceiling as if he was too scared to witness the reaction his words might have, and Harm's heart plummeted. Now he'd get chucked out. His father would apologize for the inconvenience and leave him to himself. *Where can I go? Would Angie have room for another dragon-boy?* Panic filled his heart, knowing that Blackfeather's next words would cut him to the core of his being. However, as much as he wanted to, he couldn't stop those words from coming.

Blackfeather sighed once more and spoke. "I've not been a good father for you. Not ever." He swallowed, and blinked away some tears. "Trust me, I wanted to. It hurts so much inside to know that you, of all dragons, are my son. You're so ... graceful and caring and ... manly. I couldn't wish for a better son. But I find it hard to show you how proud I am of you. I've trained myself in keeping my emotions hidden. Mordekay pounced on any weakness he found." Blackfeather's gaze returned to Harm's face. "And you always were the one reason why I didn't follow my love into death."

This was so not what Harm had expected. Fire danced in his heart and tears rolled over his face, hissing as they evaporated. He didn't know what to say. All his worries, all his fears swam away on the wave of warmth that spread through his body. He bent forward and laid his head gently on his father's chest. Blackfeather stroked his hair very carefully. Neither of them dared to speak, but for Harm, the world suddenly seemed to be a brighter place. No room in this house was as wonderful as this floral-patterned monstrosity as long as his father was sleeping in this bed.

After a while he realized that Blackfeather had fallen asleep again. Rumbling noises came from downstairs indicating that Angie had come back. Just in case it wasn't her, Harm pulled up his dragon claws, but the footsteps on the stairs were familiar.

Colin opened the door and let Angie enter first. *Ever the old-fashioned gentleman.* Harm smiled.

"Colin will look after Blackfeather for a while," Angie came right to the point. "I need your nose for the search. You know Mordekay's scent best."

"What if he comes back to finish what he started?" Harm nodded toward Blackfeather.

"I took the liberty of putting strong security spells on all the doors and windows downstairs," Angie said. "I'll do the same up here and we can go."

Harm got up. Wordlessly Colin settled into the chair he'd vacated. He waved at him with a smile but didn't talk. Harm was glad for the silence. After enchanting the window in the room, Angie went through the upper floor to secure the remaining windows.

Harm didn't have to wait long for her return, but it was enough time to process the elation he still felt. He watched every line etched into his father's face and tried to remember what his real face had looked like with its long, black hair and unmovable expression. If only he could give Blackfeather his old face back. The one he was wearing now reminded him too much of Mordekay.

"I'm ready, let's go." Angie peeked through the door, and Harm followed her. Since Mordekay's scent was all over the house, they left it and walked in a big circle around it. Luckily it wasn't a serial house. In the back, Harm picked up Mordekay's scent and pointed it out to Angie. Side by side, they followed it.

Mordekay had cut through the residential area to a busy road without a sidewalk where the obnoxious fumes from cars overlaid his scent. Angie lost it nearly immediately, but Harm had no problem sticking with it. It had etched itself into his memory. He walked away from downtown along the road with Angie in tow. Twice, a car stopped and the driver asked if he should take them along. They always shook their heads. More often, though, drivers shooting past yelled at them and shook their fists. After the third time, Harm didn't even look up any more. He was too busy tracing the scent. It led into a quieter side street just as a police car pulled up beside them.

"You're walking on a car-only road, ma'am." The officer had lowered his window but didn't bother to get out. "Please get into the car. We'll take you wherever you need to go."

"I'm sorry, but you're not needed." A thin layer of Commanding Voice threaded through Angie's words.

"We're getting off this road right now anyway," Harm tried to ease the policemen into Angie's Command. After all, they were only doing their duty. It didn't feel right to create a conflict of duty and Command in their minds. Sure, small amounts of the Commanding Voice didn't do much harm, but why risk it? He pointed to the side road, one with a sidewalk. "He went down this road."

"Are you looking for someone?" The officer's voice sounded genuinely interested.

"His dog ran away, and we're following its footprints." It was a thin lie, but Angie forced the policemen to believe it.

"Good luck." The officer's smile was friendly but a little vague. "But please remember for the next time that it is very dangerous to walk on roads without a sidewalk. Stick to the part where walking is allowed and use your car for the rest."

"Thank you for your help, officer." Harm smiled back, hoping the two men would forget about them as soon as they set their car in motion again. That often happened to people where the Commanding Voice was used for the first time. As soon as the police car drove away, he headed down the new road, followed by Angie. Since there were only a few building sites in this estate, Mordekay's scent grew stronger again and it became easier to follow it. When they reached a big, forlorn-looking patch of grass, maybe a park-to-be or a future playground, the scent ended abruptly. Harm and Angie went in ever-widening circles, but couldn't find a trace of it. His stomach seemed to fill with anxious butterflies.

"But he can't fly anymore." He stared at Angie, whose face mirrored the same shock he felt.

"A dragon must have picked him up. This is the proof that he's got an accomplice." Her voice was hoarse. "It's the only explanation."

Her words echoed through Harm's mind. What if the accomplice was knocking at their door right now and Colin, unsuspecting as he was, opened and let him in?

He turned and ran, faster than he'd ever run before, faster than any human could.

"Wait, Harm." Angie caught up with him. "I know a shortcut." Obviously she had come to the same conclusion. She took the lead, and together they raced through the suburbs. Harm was glad that most people were at work or in school. They met very few people who, looking up at the runners from what they were doing, were quick enough to spot them.

A little later, they burst through the main door and thundered up the stairs. Colin and Blackfeather, who had woken, stared at them as if they were lunatics.

"Mordekay has an accomplice," Harm burst out, panting heavily. But worse than being winded was the thought that he needed to display some of his emotions to make Blackfeather understand. "I ... I was worried about you."

A very fine smile, barely perceptible, spread over Blackfeather's face. "You were worried? About me?"

Harm blushed.

"Shouldn't we inform Lydia?" Colin sounded frightened. "If Mordekay didn't come here, he might be on his way to harm her."

"I've tried calling her," Angie said. "But she isn't answering her mobile."

"The Council probably keeps her too busy." Harm looked at his father and pulled his eyebrows up questioningly.

Blackfeather nodded. "You need to go. Angie will be able to protect me in case he shows up."

"I'm pretty sure he won't try to kill you," Colin said. "After all, you're using his body. I'm sure he'll want it back."

"Now that's an idea I hadn't even considered yet." Angie scratched her head. "I should go and talk to the Council. This is getting out of hand."

"But Mordekay's ally could be anyone." Harm frowned. "How do we know who we can trust?"

Angie bit her lip. "I promised I'd protect the future queen." She looked him in the eye. "And it doesn't sit right with me to leave the problem in the hands of a couple of teenagers, and that's what you are."

"But we have a witch on our side." Harm was glad he'd thought of that. "What if someone close to the Council is in league with Mordekay? Alerting them to the problem might end with a catastrophe."

"And for the same reason you can't go to visit Lydia." Colin looked smug. "It would alert Mordekay's ally. It's better if Harm and I go."

"You'll keep your mobiles charged and on the loudest ringtone you've got at all times." Angie's stern gaze traveled between Harm and Colin. "And you'll call me the second something goes wrong."

"Promise." Harm and Colin spoke in unison, but the worry lines never left Angie's face on the way to the forest.

TWELFTH CHAPTER

To my relief, the castle didn't look one bit like a Disney castle. Its facade, complete with turrets, windows and balconies big enough for a dragon to land on, was carved from a cliff. A huge entrance gate backed onto a big rocky platform. The whole castle reminded me of pictures of a rock town called Petra I'd seen on the Internet, except that it wasn't hidden in rocky valleys. It adorned a vertical rock face in the side of a mountain.

Awed, I set down beside the members of the Council on the rocky platform in front of the castle. A crowd of roughly a hundred dragons had gathered on the far side. I'd never seen so many in one place before, not even—as far as I remembered—when my parents were still alive. They must have sheltered me from the crowds. I stared, unbelieving, at the sea of green, brown, red, yellow, black, and copper. I even spotted a few dark blue bodies. The dragons came in many sizes from barely bigger than myself to house-sized, and all of them cheered at my arrival. Strangely enough, their elation buzzed inside my mind; a friendly welcoming hum.

Despite the welcome, a big lump stuck in my throat and I longed to be far, far away, in some remote place with Colin. Anywhere would be better than here, displayed as the future queen. I tried to swallow the lump, but that seemed impossible.

"Welcome to your rightful home." The Head of Council was a marvelous red dragon. Her voice carried over the gathered dragons that listened attentively. "We're glad you finally consented to come. Maybe we'll make a fine queen out of you yet."

I opened my mouth to protest, but one look at the hopeful, expectant faces of the gathered, and I closed it again. I couldn't deny that something tied me to every individual in the crowd, a connection or bond that made me acutely aware of the dragons that were ready to become my subjects. What would they do if they knew I'd rather be a human?

"Please, do enter. We don't have much time for your education." The Head of Council pointed to the castle.

On an impulse, I turned to the waiting dragons, bowed and said, "I'm very happy to get to know all of you. Please do have patience with me. I don't remember much from before the accident, but I'll do my best to learn as much as I can. I promise you that I will not make any rash decisions."

The applause was deafening. Rather happy with my little speech, I turned and followed the Council inside. In passing I caught a glare from the Head of Council and pressed my lips together. It wasn't my fault that my dreams differed from those of the Council.

Behind the entrance, a round ceiling with artificially smoothed walls arched over our heads. The single human standing beside a big staircase looked rather lost in the big hall.

Before I could address the human, the Head of Council grabbed my arm and pulled me around. "Why didn't you wait in the clearing for your escort like we discussed?"

"I did, but at first no one showed up, and then there came a knight and attacked me." I thought it safe to reveal that much.

"Knights are old wives' tales." The Head of Council frowned, which made the red scales on her forehead stand up nearly vertically. It was a truly strange sight. "You didn't obey, and that is not a good start for our meeting. How are we to teach you the way of dragons if you don't obey the simplest rules of honor?"

"I swear there was a knight. And he had help, some guys with clubs."

"The sort of knight that could kill a dragon died out a long, long time ago." The Head of Council's face seemed haughty, although it was hard to tell. A dragon's features were harder to read than a human's.

"Oh really?" Her superior attitude annoyed me no end, so I pulled my hind-leg forward and pointed with my snout to the gap in my scales. Although the wound had already closed, it was still red and sore enough to be clearly visible. "Do you think I cut myself just so I can tell you horror stories?"

A gasp went through the Council. I felt their worry and concern through the same bond that had connected me to all those dragons outside. Even the Head of Council seemed shocked.

"I'm sorry I didn't believe you." She turned to one Council member and ordered, "Take a flight of dragons, Telanuel, and find that knight and his supporters. There should be traces in the clearing. And if there aren't, examine the other clearings. Maybe we've got the meeting point mixed up."

The emerald green dragon nodded, turned and left without so much as a glance in my direction. I felt a pang in my heart. Wasn't I supposed to be the queen-in-the-making? Shouldn't he at least ask my permission? I shook my head. No, no. It was far better for someone else to take care of the dragons' business. It would make it easier to decline the throne. Still, a niggling flame of anger remained, so I turned my attention to the human who still stood motionless beside the staircase. Without thinking twice about it, I changed into my human form and felt each Council member's reluctance as they followed my example.

"This is Martin Longbow." The Head of Council stepped up beside me. "He'll be your personal servant and cater to every wish you have."

"I don't need a slave." Appalled, I took a step backward.

"I'm not a slave." Longbow bowed but kept looking at me. "I consider it an honor to help you get acquainted with the dragon community's quirks. Also, I know my way around very well, just in case you don't remember."

His smile was friendly and I felt safe with him.

"He will explain the basics of dragon behavior to you," the Head of Council said. "That will free our valuable time to teach you the things a queen should know. Most importantly, how to access Queen's Magic."

A little voice inside my head whispered, *That's something that can't be taught. Be careful what you say.* Was that my mother or my father or maybe both of them?

I didn't know, but I decided to heed the warning. "Can we leave the learning till tomorrow? I just arrived and would like to get used to the place."

"That's a reasonable request," one of the other Council members said. His smile was fleeting but friendly and there was a twinkle in his eyes that made me like him instantly. "Maybe roaming these halls will bring back some memories."

The Head of Council's mouth was a pencil-thin line, but she nodded her approval. "We will see you tomorrow morning then." In the blink of an eye, she'd turned back into her dragon form and walked past me, up the stairs. The other Council members said their farewells before they, too, turned into dragons and left through the big entrance, until only my bodyguard and the supportive dragon remained. Longbow didn't say a word. The dragon was more talkative.

"By the way, my name's Herbert." His human body was rather short and a little bent. He seemed quite old to me, at least eighty—by human standards; who knew how old he really was? I still hadn't figured out the relation between human and dragon time. "This place is huge, and one day isn't much time to explore. I suggest you start with the library."

Ma parents filled my heart with the certainty that his words were not only wise but that the library was exactly the place I needed to go to. "Thank you for the advice."

"You're welcome. I'm sure you'll find plenty of interesting facts there." He winked at me again, turned without changing his form, and walked away. At the entrance, he turned once more and made a shooing motion, before he exited.

I wasted a few more minutes staring after him. Did that mean I had a friend in the Council? That could be really helpful. I turned to Longbow. "Do you know where the library is?"

"Sure, but it's off limits for any dragon below the level of maturity."

"Even if it's the future queen?"

"I have not been given differing information." His smooth, light brown features were nearly as hard to read as those of a dragon.

"And what does maturity mean?" Maybe there was a way around this strange rule.

"A dragon reaches maturity when it bonds." This time there seemed to be a flicker of warmth in his smile.

I relaxed. "I have bonded a while ago."

"You did?" The surprise on his face was so worth it.

"Angie can testify to it. Do you want to call her?" I pulled my mobile from my pocket, but he shook his head.

"I can easily test it right here. If you would follow me, please?" He pointed to a small doorway left of the stairs. When I hesitated, he added, "The library is that way too."

So I followed him along a dimly lit corridor that led deeper into the mountain. Twice it had other corridors splitting off, but we stayed on the main route. It ended in a small chamber, also rounded, which made it look more like a cave. A bed of red gold covered half of the ground. I knew what dragons used the gold for, but why would Longbow take me to a bedroom?

"What's this for?" My curiosity got the better of me. I walked toward the gold and picked up a small figurine. It resembled a kitten but had a fishtail instead of hind legs.

"One of your ancestors tied a spell to its hoard. Anyone near it is forced to speak the truth." He leaned against the wall. "Go ahead, try lying."

"My name is Ni… Ni…" No matter how I tried, the name 'Nicole' just didn't leave my mouth. It was as if something in my mind forced me to pull it back. And the gold's warm glow dulled to an angry red that the human obviously must be able to see, considering his wide grin. So I concluded the sentence with my real name, and the gold looked like before, warm and inviting.

"Now that the purpose of this room has been established, do you still claim you've bonded?" His eyebrows rose but it seemed to be genuine curiosity rather than mistrust.

"I have bonded. My heart belongs to someone, and it will never be free again." I felt quite smug that I'd managed to tell the truth without giving away Colin's name. The gold's hue remained unchanged, and there was even a little echo in my mind that suggested that my ancestor, the inventor of this chamber, was approving of my choice of Colin. Could that be possible? I would need to talk to my parents. But not now and not here, with a stranger looking at me as if I was the most eccentric sight his eyes had ever met.

"What are we waiting for?" I said. "Let's go to the library."

He left the room with an expression stuck between awe and puzzlement. Still, he took me to the library. The corridors leading there were so twisted and had so many intersections and staircases that I was sure I'd never find the way there again, but my parents assured me I would never have problems getting around the castle. I always forgot that I wasn't alone, and each reminder warmed my heart.

To my surprise, the library was a rectangular room with wooden shelves and big windows showing the rock platform in front of the castle. To my surprise, a lot of the dragons were still there, standing together in small groups, chatting, and—from the looks of it—ready to spend a lot more time there. My heart went out to them. Were they really willing to remain in the cold just to see their queen again? *Their potential queen,* I reminded myself. *Maybe I should tell them to go home, at least for the time being.*

I stepped inside the library and discovered that the stony ground was warm to the touch. Immediately my mind turned away from the gathered dragons. What was it that I couldn't help thinking about them? The warm stone slabs of the ground explained why the room was so dry—I guess it was necessary to protect all those books and scrolls on the shelves.

"The library is heated from below." Longbow must have interpreted my surprised look correctly. "Damp walls are a hazard for the valuable scripts, but open fires would have been too dangerous. So the architects adapted something they'd learned from the Romans. Your bedchamber is heated like that too."

That was good news. I just hoped they'd have a real bed too and not just a pile of gold. I'd grown accustomed to sleeping in my human form. But right now, the library was more important. "Is there a system or a digital catalog?"

"Digital?" He laughed, and it sounded far more human than anything I'd heard from him this far. "The minute I catch one of the dragons in charge with a digital gadget is the time I start believing in unicorns and dragon-killing knights."

"Well, lucky you. That time has come now, hasn't it?" I grinned and held up my mobile.

"You're not in charge. Not yet." His features became stern again. "And by all I've heard you're not interested in ever taking up the job anyway."

Another pang shot through my heart. Why was it suddenly so painful to follow my dream? The dragons would never accept Colin for their king, and I would surely be more at home with the humans. "Well, do they have something like a catalog?"

"There's a register on the table over there." He pointed to a high desk beside the door. "I don't know if it'll help though."

Anything that made it easier to find the scrolls or books I needed would help. I walked over, opened the thin, leather-bound book, and stared unbelievingly at the scratching on the page. What kind of writing was that? Although it did seem oddly familiar, I couldn't make out a single letter. My confusion must have been obvious.

"It's Draconish, the language of the dragons. All the texts in the library are written in it. I thought you were familiar with it." He shrugged without looking at me. It gave him an apologetic air.

"Is there a book around that'll help me learn it?" I bit my lip to keep the frustration from turning into anger. It wasn't Longbow's fault that the books weren't written in a script I could read.

He shook his head. "It's all in the minds of dragons only. I'm sorry to say, but I can't read it either. They only teach it to dragons. I guess they still don't trust my tribe despite our centuries of servitude."

"Centuries of servitude?" That didn't sound good at all to me.

He shrugged again. "It's a long story."

"Well, since I can't yet use the library, you might as well show me to my room and tell me all about it." I turned with all the determination I could muster and walked out of the library. When Longbow followed me, I heard him suppress a chuckle. At the next intersection, he passed me and took the lead. At the same time, he told me of the day the dragons had come to America.

"The way our ancestors tell the story is sacred, so I can only give you a condensed version." With his back to me, he marched through the corridors, obviously expecting me to keep up with him. "Many, many suns ago, one of our chiefs, guarded by ten of his most stalwart warriors, was sitting on a rock overlooking the prairie plains, contemplating the future of our tribe. Our lands were rich with plenty of buffalo and edible plants. The big problem was that we'd been at war with our neighbors for many suns. Our people had dwindled from many hundreds to but a few scores. Regardless how well our warriors fought, the other tribes' raiders stole our women, enslaved our children, killed our men, and invaded our territory whenever they could.

"The chief knew we'd need allies, but there were no tribes we could turn to. So he was sitting on his rock pondering the problem when he saw a cloud of what he thought were enormous birds. But they weren't birds. The closer they came, the better he could make out their colors and shapes, their incredible muscles and the serrated teeth in their mouths. Once in a while, one of the 'birds' swooped down and caught a whole buffalo, carrying it off without much struggle.

"The chief thought these newcomers were the fabled Thunderbird, so he fell to his knees and called to the their leader. To his surprise, they swerved and landed on the plains below him. Only the most beautiful one landed beside him on the rocky outcrop.

"'What do you want,' she said right into his head and in a language he understood.

"'Help us against our enemies.' He held up his hands. 'Help us in our need and we'll do whatever you want us to do.'

"The dragon queen, for that was who she was, studied him, his warriors, and their stone axes and spears. Although his men trembled with fear, none showed anything but reverence. 'Methinks this meeting was one of chance and luck for both of us,' she finally said. 'For we have come a long, long way to find a new home, and your lands seem suitable. But we also came to get away from people, and people there are a lot of.'

"My anc… I mean … the chief dared to get up. He bowed and said, 'If you drive away the raiders and help my tribe in our need, we will protect you forever and a day. No other people will ever grace these lands but the ones in my tribe.'

"Thus, a pact was formed. The dragons put a spell on this mountain range and the surrounding prairie that kept away all humans, and my tribe has been their servants ever since. We helped them shape the castle without understanding why anyone would need an underground place this big. We cooked for them, for they took to eating cooked meals rather quickly, cleaned their scales for them, something especially our children enjoyed, and helped them collect enough of the yellow metal they needed for their nests. We even fought at their side when the white man came. Their illusions made our fighters seem far more dangerous than they were, and whole armies fled from us. In the end, the white people declared our lands a reservation and forgot all about us. And that's just the way we want it." Longbow opened a wooden door, big enough for a dragon. "Here's your room."

Instead of stepping through, I asked, "Are you happy serving the dragons?"

Longbow shrugged. "For the most part, the dragons are good to us. Some even consider us friends."

"Like Herbert?"

"Like Herbert." His face was solemn but there was a look in his eyes that suggested to me that he was closer to Herbert than he'd let on.

Thinking of Blackfeather's experience, I asked, "What if a dragon treated you like a slave?"

"There are a few dragons who consider us inferior and treat us accordingly." His face took on a guarded expression.

"However, no one works for a megalomaniac dragon like that for long. The Council takes complaints very seriously."

"A human can't complain if the dragon used the Commanding Voice on him, though." I needed to understand why no dragon and no 'servant' had ever noticed Blackfeather's distress.

Longbow's eyes widened. "No dragon would dare. The Head of Council would find out and punish the deed severely. It'd be a duel to the death where the challenged dragon wouldn't stand a chance. After all, the Head of Council wields the most magic of any dragon beside the queen!"

"I see." I walked past him lost in thought. Why hadn't the Head of Council ever noticed the way Mordekay had treated Blackfeather? I certainly needed to talk to her.

When I bumped against a footstool beside a fireplace, the pain ripped me from my pondering. I turned in a circle and looked around. A big four-poster bed stood in the middle of the room, right beside a big pile of gold. Close to the window that led to a balcony stood a big wardrobe that nonetheless seemed rather lost in the giant room. I longed to go back to my parents' house. There were so many complications.

"Ah, there you are." In her dragon form, the Head of Council swept past Longbow, impatience in her voice. "You're needed in the throne room. But first, show yourself to your subjects. They've been waiting patiently." She waved to the window with a paw. For reasons I couldn't explain, I turned into my dragon form obediently, stood on the balcony for a while, and let the applause wash over me. I frowned. Now, why had I done this? I didn't really want to be stared at by hundreds of dragons, did I?

As I followed Longbow and the Head of Council through the corridors, I wondered about my strange reaction.

Thirteenth Chapter

*H*arm felt crushed between the two burly dragons walking on either side of him and longed to be someplace else, preferably close to where Nicole was. The crowd outside the castle had growled at him and Colin, and the corridors on the way to the throne room weren't wide enough for three dragons side by side. The cold disapproval of the dragons so far also didn't help him to relax. He'd known they wouldn't be too happy to see him again, but why didn't they allow him to change back into his human form? He didn't dare to complain though. Maybe it'd been Lydia's order. Secretly he'd always feared that she would change her mind about becoming queen the minute she felt the natural connection of dragonkind.

"Walk up to the throne." The bigger of his companions pushed him forward.

"And don't dare to misbehave." The second one glared first at him and then at Colin.

Harm stumbled forward along an alley of light, barely aware of Colin's weight between his shoulder blades. Each pair of columns he passed bore six candles. The rest of the throne room was shrouded in darkness. He couldn't even make out the ceiling.

"What's going on?" Colin whispered.

"I don't know." Harm tried to pierce the darkness in the gigantic cave, but that proved impossible despite his dragon eyes. He felt that quite a lot of dragons were present, but how many exactly he couldn't say. As they neared the end, the breathing of two dragons and a human reached his ear. At the last pair of columns, light flared up at the front of the room to reveal a raised dais with two thrones made of gold. They resembled tables more than chairs because they had been created for dragons resting on them. An impossibly long curtain of red velvet hung from the ceiling behind the thrones. And in front of them, a blood red and a white dragon stood beside a sun-tanned young man.

"Harm! Colin!" Lydia's voice sounded surprised and happy. Maybe she hadn't been brainwashed yet after all? She took a step forward, but the Head of Council held her back and whispered something into her ear.

A vertical frown appeared on Lydia's white scaled face. "Harm is no traitor. It's something I just don't believe." She shrugged off the Head of Council's paw and turned back into human form. Then she hurried toward her friends.

"Why am I here?" Harm looked at the Head of Council for an answer. Had they found out that Nicole was a witch and that he'd helped her discover it? They wouldn't be very pleased if they still considered witches to be in league with humans. With trembling paws, he helped Colin from his back while he waited for the old, blood red dragon to explain.

"You are accused of having attacked our queen on—"

"Potential queen," Lydia interrupted her.

132

The Head of Council shot her an angry look, but corrected herself. "Our potential queen on her way to the castle. You conspired with Mordekay and dressed up as a knight to murder her before she could fulfill her destiny. The young men who helped you were diagnosed positively with dragon magic."

Harm's jaw dropped and he froze mid-move, staring at the Head of Council. All thoughts of Nicole vanished temporarily from his mind. Someone had attacked Lydia? But that wasn't possible. Mordekay had flown away, together with whomever his accomplice was. The bigger issue took longer to reach his mind. They were accusing *him*?

"You are hereby sentenced to exile." A hard-to-interpret ripple tugged at the corners of the Head of Council's mouth. "To emphasize our generosity, you are allowed to take along provisions and whatever you can carry of your possessions. You—"

"This is ridiculous." Again Lydia interrupted the Head of Council. She counted off her criticism on her fingers. "First, Harm would never, ever do anything that might be dangerous to me."

Harm appreciated her fervor, but knew that a verdict, once spoken, would not be revoked. His heart grew leaden and all the tiny little flames that normally danced through his body died. He didn't mind leaving the dragon society if they didn't want him, but how could he stay close to Nicole if he had to leave?

But Lydia wasn't done yet. "Second, he's not even had a real trial. You simply announced what he's supposed to have done without giving any proof whatsoever. Third, you can no longer rule as if you're the queen. You keep insisting that I have to 'fulfill my destiny' but you simply make decisions for me. So if you're earnest about training me as the future queen, you will have to let me handle situations like this, at least for the time I'm here." She folded her arms in front of her chest, riding out the many sighs and gasps from the hidden audience before she continued. "And last, there's a perfectly easy way to find out if Harm was the knight or not."

Was there? A flicker of hope sparked in Harm's chest. If the queen-to-be intervened on his behalf, maybe there was a way out of his banishment.

"And what would that be? Do you think one of them technical gadgets caught the knight dressing up?" The Head of Council's voice dripped disdain.

"No. And even if it did, I'm sure you would refuse to accept it as proof." Lydia held out her hand to Harm. "Come on, Harm, turn into a human so I can interrogate you."

Confused, Harm did as he'd been told.

"Anyone who wants to come can do so, but only in their human form or there won't be enough room." Lydia spoke to the hidden audience again. "We will need at least a couple of witnesses, so feel free to come." She took his hand and walked toward an exit behind the two huge golden thrones and the curtain. Harm heard the rustling of wings as dragons changed, the mourning sighs when they adapted to the unwanted form, and the shuffling of feet. Obviously most of the dragons were too curious to ignore Lydia's invitation.

With a long trail of dragons-turned-human in tow they traveled the corridors in silence. Harm wondered about Lydia's certainty of the path. How did she know her way around so well? After all, she'd only been here a few hours.

They reached a mid-sized room with a huge hoard of gold that glowed slightly.

"As all of you should remember," Lydia said, "dragons cannot lie, but they can keep part of the truth for themselves, which can create lies too. I guess that's the reason my ancestor bespelled this gold. It forces dragons to tell the truth. And maybe humans too, but we still need to test that. In either case, the trick is to ask the right questions. Let's begin." She turned to Harm. "Tell us what Mordekay is to you, and try to lie."

Harm's mind scrambled for something he could say without getting into trouble. "Mordekay's my fa…" The word 'father' didn't make it past his lips, although he knew that under normal circumstances he could have used it. After all, Mordekay had posed as his father long enough to make it partially true. Still, he found it impossible to claim Mordekay as his father. It wasn't true enough. At his next try, the gold lit up with an angry, red glow. He stared at Lydia with surprise. How had she learned of this room?

"There. You can see what happens if he tries to lie," Lydia said. "Now, tell us. Have you been conspiring with Mordekay?"

Harm bit his lip. He felt the truth rising, and it was impossible to keep it from pouring out. "Yes, I did. We tried to make you fall in love with me before any other dragon got the chance, so you'd choose me to be your king. Mordekay thought he could gain influence that way."

The gold's glow returned to normal. *This is the best lie detector ever,* he thought.

"Why have you changed your mind?" Lydia sounded genuinely interested.

"You were so…" Harm searched for the right word and tried again. "You made me look at the world in a different light. And when Mordekay attempted to take over my body to force the

135

binding between us, I could no longer do his bidding. You're too good a friend to betray your trust."

"Did you dress up as a knight to kill me?" Lydia grinned reassuringly at him, as if she already knew the answer.

"No, and if I get my paws on the culprit, I'll peel him from his protective cover and rip him apart." Harm hadn't known how deep his anger about the attack sat. A wave of sympathy washed through him and it took him a while to realize that it came from the other dragons.

"Did you hire or Command a knight to attack me?"

"No." Harm ground his teeth.

"I'm sure Mordekay is trying to frame him for this." Colin spoke for the first time. "I would expect Mordekay to try to get his revenge on Lydia, and hiring a knight is just the kind of thing he'd do."

Harm held his breath. Dragons did not appreciate human interference, especially when it came to trials, but before anyone could react, Lydia winked at Colin and went on questioning Harm, pretending that nothing had happened.

"Did you hire or Command a group of humans to help a knight kill me?" She seemed determined to wash him off any lingering suspicion.

"No."

"Are you loyal to the crown or to me?"

He hadn't expected this question, and it required him to think for a while. "I am loyal to you, Lydia. If you decide not to remain with dragonkind, if you decide to spend the rest of your life as a human, I'll be at your side."

Every human-turned-dragon held their breath, waiting for a reaction from Lydia, but she just smiled at him and turned to the Head of Council, who was now a woman in a long, white robe with hair as black as a raven's wing hanging to her waist. "As you can see, your assumptions were wrong. Harm neither pretended to be a knight nor did he hire one. It is far more likely that Mordekay is behind the scheme. Therefore the verdict you so casually announced is wrong. Will you withdraw it?"

The red dragon looked as if it had swallowed a living, fighting cat without chewing. "I stand corrected and apologize to you, Harm. The verdict is void." She turned to a bearded human. "Telanuel, why has no one ever thought about using this room as a truth chamber?" She didn't wait for an answer. "Set out and find the real knight. If this room works for humans too, we need to interrogate him in here. It's imperative that we find the person or persons behind the attack, and the knight is bound to know." She turned back to Lydia. "Thank you for alerting us to the usefulness of this room. We've been debating dismantling it for quite a while, never thinking about how useful it could be." She bowed to Lydia. "Please do remind me from time to time that an outside view can be surprisingly efficient." Then she turned and walked out of the room swiftly, obviously intent on some task only she knew about. Some of the watchers, including the man she'd addressed as Telanuel, followed her.

A sudden burst of clapping and cheering made Harm gaze around. There were smiles on most faces. Unbidden, Nicole's features appeared in his mind. Did this really mean he'd get a chance to prove to her that she could rely on him, always?

An elderly, slightly stooped man put his hand on his shoulder. "Congratulations, young man." He smiled a toothless smile. "Now make sure no one will get to the queen while she's here. Longbow is a good man but he's no match for a dragon."

FOURTEENTH CHAPTER

*T*he trial had been hard for Colin. He'd so wanted to help Lydia and Harm, but the one time he spoke he'd realized pretty fast that the dragons weren't prepared to listen to a human. He wouldn't forget the angry gazes some of them had thrown at him any time soon.

That did not bode well for his love for Lydia. The dragons would never accept a human at the side of their queen. And maybe they were right. He watched Lydia handle the situation like a true queen. She was so calm and self-assured, his heart widened with pride. She'd be the best queen the dragons ever had. How could he demand she give this up? Especially since he was nothing but a human, where the males weren't exactly known for lifelong fidelity. If only ... if only he could be the man Lydia needed at her side.

Just as the last witnesses left the chamber, she caught his gaze, came over and kissed him wordlessly. Electrical currents ran through his body, something he'd never experienced before with the few girlfriends he'd had. How could he give her up when she meant more to him than the world? When she let go of him, he noticed the Native American waiting silently in the background, deliberately not looking in their direction.

"He's my bodyguard," Lydia whispered, pulling him back toward the corridors. "And a guide around the castle. You'll see, the place is huge."

"Does that ice cold she-dragon, the red one, live here too?" Colin knew he didn't want to share a roof with that one.

"You mean the Head of Council?" Lydia turned to the young man who was walking beside Harm. "Does she, Longbow?"

"Rutabella Draconia moved into the west wing the day she was elected Head of Council." The young man's face was as inexpressive as Blackfeather's had been when he had still been in his own body. Did they train this? Colin remembered reading something like that about Native Americans.

Lydia stopped and looked along one of the intersections. "Say, is there a human-sized room in this mess?"

"Naturally." Longbow bowed slightly. "It is a reception room with a small kitchen. I can make you some coffee or other refreshments."

"That'd be delightful. Show the way."

Colin felt a pang of jealousy when she smiled at Longbow, but he forced it down. She'd said that she were in love with him, and Angie had sworn that dragons only loved once. There was no need to be jealous. Still, watching her walk beside the young man chatting amiably caused his hands to curl into fists.

"Say," Harm accosted Lydia, "where's Nicole?"

"I left her at my parents' house. She was…" Lydia hesitated a moment, "very tired. I thought the two of you might prefer staying there with her." She made it sound like a question. Did she want to get rid of him? Colin fought down another wave of jealousy. Lydia would never send him away if it wasn't important.

"I'd visit you every day after my lessons." She rolled her eyes. "I'm expecting them to be rather boring, but I need to show them my goodwill. There's something … I can't really explain it … it's like a bond between the dragons and me. I can't just let them down."

Colin's mouth went dry. "Does that mean you will become their queen?" That'd definitely be the end of their relationship. He didn't know whether to cry or to be secretly relieved that he'd never get into a situation where he might accidentally hurt her feelings.

"No, silly." Lydia turned around and put her arms around his neck, kissing him a couple of times in the process. "But I can't just leave without finding someone suitable to take my place."

A whole mountain of worry crumbled from Colin's heart only to be replaced by a different kind of worry. Would it always be like this? Would he only be able to enjoy the moments when he felt her arms around him? He smiled as best he could and kissed her back.

Longbow cleared his throat. "The room you requested is right in front of us. It might be a little more comfortable there."

Harm huffed, clearly trying to fight down his laugh.

Hand in hand Colin and Lydia followed them to a small rectangular room with a low ceiling and human-sized furniture. The room wasn't very lavish but the table with four seats would do, and the pictures on the wall were nice enough to make the room seem cozy. Within a few minutes, Longbow had a fire dancing in the fireplace and milk warming on the stove in the kitchen beside the room.

"You know, I've been thinking about this attacker ever since my flight." Lydia sat on a chair and leaned back. It surprised Colin that she didn't talk about anything more important like

Mordekay and his plans. She scratched her nose. "I know I smelled him before, I just can't remember for the life of me where it was. His scent was flowery, bordering on the feminine. But I'm sure it was a man. A young one. Does that ring any bells?"

Harm shrugged. "The whole school is full of young men, and the scent you noticed could have been from his girlfriend or from the detergent he uses for his laundry. Also, he doesn't really have to be in our school."

"True. I just thought it strange." Lydia closed her eyes as if she was trying to remember something. "There wasn't much time during the fight, but I am quite sure I've met this knight before. If only I could remember, I'd be better prepared the next time he shows up."

Colin frowned. "Surely a single knight wouldn't be so stupid and come to the lair of a whole bunch of dragons on his own."

"If he's with Mordekay, he won't be on his own," Harm pointed out. "And two humans can hide very well from the dragons."

Lydia sighed. "Why does life have to be so complicated?"

"Hot chocolate, like you requested," Longbow announced as he entered the room from the kitchen, carrying a tray with three mugs.

Lydia's eyebrows rose. "Aren't you going to drink a mug too?"

For a split second, Longbow's face relaxed with surprise, which made him look much younger and very vulnerable, then he caught himself. "It wouldn't be decent for a servant."

"Bollocks!"

Colin suppressed a grin. Lydia would never be someone who took decency for an excuse.

"Get yourself a mug and sit down with us," she ordered. "We need to figure out how I can learn to read dragon script so I can comb through the manuscript to find a suitable replacement."

Nicole spent most of her day on the sofa, either sleeping or telling White Crow what had happened in the last few months. After eating another big meal in the afternoon, she felt refreshed and ready to get up and finally *do* something. She wanted to be prepared when Lydia came back. Also, any activity would take her mind off Harm. The way his face usurped her thoughts at the most inappropriate moments was annoying. When White Crow looked in on her once more, she asked, "Can you teach me right now how to use my magic without running into a food problem again?"

White Crow laughed but the merriness was mixed with sadness. "As I said, I'm no magician and no witch. I only know what I read and discussed with some of the dragons I once called friends."

"I'd take anything as long as it keeps me from starving to death every time I use magic." Nicole was surprised how easily she accepted the fact that she'd used magic twice already. During her forced break she'd decided that it didn't help worrying over whether she was going nuts or not. Either she already was crazy—in which case she had Lydia and Harm to share her mental state with—or she truly was a witch, in which case she'd have to come to terms with her abilities anyway. So she might as well learn as much as she could before Lydia showed up again. The only thing she feared was telling Colin and her parents, for she could not keep something this big from them. But it was nothing she would have to think about right now.

"There's a nice, blue sky outside. Let's see if you can manage to pull some energy from the sun." White Crow took her hand and helped her to her feet. To her surprise, she still felt a little wobbly, but when she followed him into the forest, her weakness faded.

White Crow found them a spot where a single tree had fallen, creating just about enough room for the sunshine to reach the forest floor. He told her to stand in the middle of the sunny patch. "Stand with your face to the sun," he said, "and close your eyes. Feel the warmth on your skin. Let it fill your mouth as if it is a nicely flavored drink."

Nicole did her best to comply, but nothing happened. She giggled. As if anyone could drink sunshine.

"If you truly want to learn, you will need to trust my advice even if it will take you a while to learn." White Crow's voice was warm and low. "Concentrate on the sunshine."

The whole idea seemed crazy to Nicole. However, if she could call a unicorn from wherever, why shouldn't it be possible to drink sunshine? She closed her eyes, opened her mouth, and imagined the sun rays as liquid warmth. To her surprise, the warmth filled her mouth immediately, running over her lips and face, washing away any lingering doubt she'd still had. Yes, she was a witch. She felt it in her bones. And the crazy sister of her grandmother had been one too; she just didn't have the luck to run into someone who understood.

All of a sudden, the sun's warmth reminded her of Harm's steady belief in her. He'd always been ready to help, regardless of how badly she'd treated him. He was a true friend. She swallowed, and the sun's warmth combined with the warm feeling she got from thinking of Harm filled her stomach, spread through her body, and strengthened her limbs. She felt it tingle in her fingers, so she opened her eyes and looked over to White Crow.

"I think I've got plenty already," she said. "Now that I swallowed the energy, what do I do with it?"

"You swallowed it?" His face paled. "I'm not sure that's such a good idea."

"What do dragons do with it then?" Nicole wasn't worried. Something deep inside of her knew that it wasn't dangerous for her to store the energy in her body this way. She'd just taken in a little too much.

"They roll it into a small ball that they keep under their tongue for later use." White Crow came closer, scratching his beardless chin and always keeping a tree between them as if she might explode any minute. "How does it feel?"

Nicole smiled. It was the first lighthearted smile since the incident with the black dragon. "It's all fine. I just think I swallowed a little too much. My fingers are tingling."

"Try a spell. Something small," he suggested.

"But I don't know any spells. That's part of the problem." If she hadn't felt so utterly happy and relaxed, Nicole would have stomped her foot.

"I wish I could give you some draconian spells, but I never paid much attention to them." White Crow scratched his chin again. "Can't you make one up? Maybe one that creates a small ball of light on your palm. That's one dragonets learn first when they start their education."

"Can all dragons do magic?" Nicole cocked her head waiting for the answer while, at the same time, she pondered the problem of how to create a light in broad daylight.

"Instinctively." He stepped out from behind the tree. "But they need to learn the spells to focus their magic or it won't do what they want it to do. Also it would eat up their strength in no time if they didn't learn how to use energy that doesn't come from their bodies. I've seen dragonets do some spectacular things before they understood the basics." He sighed. "I think I'll have to contact an old friend. You'll need to learn dragon script so you can read through the right books in the library."

"Wouldn't that be forbidden?"

"Oh yes, very." He grinned at her and it made her feel daring, even a little cheeky. "But most dragons don't like to read, so it's rarely used. Now, what are you going to do about that surplus of energy?"

Nicole shrugged. The tingling in her fingers had grown into an unpleasant sensation that reminded her of the time she'd pricked herself with a needle—only this was a whole box of needles pricking her fingertips. She knew she didn't have much time before the surplus spilled out, hurting her in the process and doing strange things to White Crow and their surroundings. Panic surged through her.

She bit her lip and did her best to fight it back. *It's going to be fine,* she told herself. *There's still time to figure something out.*

"There are so many seedlings around here." White Crow pointed to the ground. "What if you send some of the energy into one? If you focus the magic well enough, all it will do is let it grow a little."

"And if I don't focus it well?" She looked at him. "I think it's probably best if you leave. Find a place where I can't harm you accidentally."

White Crow hesitated, clearly determined to help her, but she made shooing motions with her hands and he obeyed. She closed her eyes and felt for the seedlings. In her mind, she felt them like little lanterns of life.

"Grow," she said to the smallest one and tried to let the magic flow from her fingers. It didn't work. With all her might, she pushed, and the magic spilled out of her in all directions. She had to reel it in before it harmed anyone. She imagined a lasso of sunlight and caught the stray threads. Bundling them into a powerful stream, she aimed it at the tiny seedling. "Grow and be beautiful."

Whoosh!

She stepped back hurriedly, opening her eyes wide, as the seedling grew to a full-sized fir tree in the matter of minutes. Her knees buckled and her stomach cramped. She'd overdosed and used some of her own strength again. Hurriedly, she opened her mouth once more and drank a little more of the sun's warmth. Then she held her breath. The hunger pang was gone, as was the tingling pain in her fingertips. Had she found the right balance? Only time would tell. She glanced up at the tree. Wow!

"I am impressed." White Crow had returned and put a hand on her shoulder, staring up at the tree too. "You're a very talented and powerful witch. I'm glad you're on our side. By the way, we've got visitors you might like to see."

"Is Lydia back?"

"Yes, and she brought a couple of friends."

They returned to the house and Nicole's heart danced a small, happy dance when she saw Harm standing beside her brother. The young dragon bowed to her and looked extremely pleased. She blushed and turned to Lydia to hide her confusion. She'd better concentrate on the important things.

"Do you know how I can learn dragon script?" she asked. "White Crow thinks I need to read a couple of books from the dragons' library so I can learn the spells I'll need."

146

"You're not the only one who needs to learn the script." Lydia told her about the library and her hope to find a hopefully mostly up-to-date genealogical tree.

White Crow nodded at her. "The Head of Council will have someone teach you, but Nicole is a human. No dragon will teach her openly. Especially not if they realize how powerful a witch she is." He sank down onto the sofa with a sigh. "I had hoped to avoid contacting anyone yet, but it seems I must ask Herbert. He's a good teacher and probably the only one willing to help."

"Surely Angie would teach us if we asked," Harm said. Nicole noticed White Crow flinch at the name. Could he be … no, that wasn't possible, was it?

Colin nodded. "We could ask her when she brings Blackfeather here."

"She can't!" White Crow seemed surprisingly pale to Nicole. "They'll take Blackfeather for Mordekay and sentence him right away."

"In that case we'll have to smuggle him here and you can keep him hidden," Lydia said. This time even she seemed to notice the thin line of White Crow's lips because she asked, "Why are you so determined that no one knows you're still alive?" She sat beside him. "I mean, the dragons know that Mordekay tried to kill me, and his accomplice is with him. It's not as if either can harm you."

"It's not about me. I don't care if I get hurt…" White Crow got up with a jerk. "Well, it's extremely unlikely that Herbert is the culprit. And the faster we reveal him, the better for Blackfeather and for you." He left the room with a nod to all.

"He's so lonely." Lydia stared after him. "I wish I could do something for him."

Nicole looked around. Had no one but her noticed the strange reaction he'd shown when Angie had been mentioned?

"I think I'd better head back to the castle." Lydia got up as well and hugged Colin. "Longbow won't be able to keep my absence a secret when dinnertime rolls around. I know you'll be safe here."

Together with Harm and Colin, Nicole waved Lydia goodbye as her friend took her dragon form and flew away, a white streak in an ever-darkening sky.

Fifteenth Chapter

After dinner, Nicole lay on her bed in her bedroom staring at the ceiling, daydreaming, when a timid knock on the door made her sit up. "Come in." She expected Colin or White Crow, but it was Harm who entered her room.

He didn't look at her. "I just wanted to make sure you're alright. Lydia told us about your…" His voice trailed off.

"It's okay. I've accepted who I am, but I'm still untrained, so I overdid my first spell a bit." She tried to smile reassuringly, not knowing whether she was successful. It was the hardest thing not to jump him and hug him. He might misunderstand and think she were in love with him. And he'd been such a steadfast friend, she didn't want to lose that.

"Oh, good." He looked up. "Do the spells in the book I gave you help with your training? It's the only book Mordekay owned that wasn't in dragon script."

"Oh dear, I completely forgot about that book." Nicole slid off the bed and went to her wardrobe. The book still peeked out of the pocket of her jacket that hung lonely in the big space. "I should read through it and learn the spells by heart."

"I could help you, if you want." There was an eagerness in Harm's tone that made Nicole's heart beat faster. "Some of them were the first spells I learned too."

"That'd be nice." She couldn't believe she'd said that. Her ears felt as hot as if they'd been burned by the sun. She grabbed the book and returned to her bed. Harm joined her and peeked over her shoulder as she flipped through the pages. His breath hit her cheek, which increased the heat in her ears. She found it really hard to concentrate on the words, her pulse was pounding so hard.

"There, that's an easy one." Harm pointed at a page. "I used it for hide and seek games until the other kids didn't want to play with me anymore because I always found them."

It said, 'The Trackinge Spelle' and seemed pretty straightforward. All she needed was her imagination, an item—anything would do—and the word written in the middle of the page. She looked around for something she could use.

With a smile, Harm twisted the round handle of her nightstand's drawer until it came off and handed it to her. "I hide and you'll find me."

Her heart beat even faster, if that was possible, when she took the knob and closed her eyes. It was extremely easy to call up Harm's picture in her mind. Truth be told, it was too easy. When had she ever paid so much attention to how he looked? Had she ever consciously noticed the little dimples when he smiled? Or the twinkle in his eyes whenever he looked at her? She breathed deeply to calm her racing heart and hoped Harm would consider the sigh as a sign of nervousness.

"Keep your eyes closed and try to remember the way I look." He sounded so reassuring. Nicole was sure that with him she'd always be safe. It was good to have a friend like that. His voice had a calming effect on her. "Say the word when I'm gone. The knob will light up and pull you in the right direction. Did you understand everything?"

She nodded, keeping his picture in her mind like a beacon. The bed creaked and his hand patted her shoulder once. Then the door clicked, once for open and then closed. She gave him a few more seconds to hide.

"Mechadjidj," she said and held her breath. To her surprise she didn't feel any more hungry than before. Maybe using the right spellwords stopped her from overdoing it. She opened her eyes. For a fleeting second, she was disappointed that Harm wasn't sitting beside her anymore. Hurriedly she got up and held the knob toward the door. It lit up with a dull yellow shine, and a gentle tug urged her toward the door. She turned to the window and the knob stopped glowing. However, its pull increased. So it seemed to work.

She walked out the door, following the glow and pull of her knob, wondering if it'd follow Harm on its own if she let go of it. It led her out of the house and into the forest where its light was the only illumination she had. Strangely enough she wasn't scared. The night was peaceful with barely any sound.

With one hand stretched out so she'd feel obstacles early enough to evade them, she turned this way and that, always choosing the path where her light and the pull were the strongest. It was a neat spell, but she hoped she'd find Harm soon. There, hadn't that been breathing? But it was behind her, and her knob was still pulling her forward. Before she could turn, a hand covered her mouth and an arm dragged her backward. She struggled in vain against the attacker, whose body pressed against hers as he pulled her along.

She lost her knob, which rolled away still glowing. The forest suddenly looked sinister. Nicole shuddered.

"Stop struggling." The whisper came from right beside her ear. "I'm not going to hurt you."

Nicole didn't listen and tried to grab behind her.

"Stop it, I said. You're not a dragon, so you don't need to be afraid." The attacker jerked her around and his hand slipped off Nicole's mouth. She debated calling for help but feared he'd pulled her too far from the house already. Well, Harm would come after her the second he realized she wasn't going to find him. The thought of her friend calmed her enough to ask, "What do you want?"

"You're close to the dragon queen." The whisper was so low that it was impossible to tell whether the speaker was male or female. "Help me to kill her, and we can rid the world of the monsters once and for all. Dragons are lost without their queen."

"Are you nuts?" Nicole struggled against the grip again. "They're my friends."

"They turn humans into slaves." The grip became tighter. Nicole felt the strength in the arm, but also a certain tenderness in the way the attacker made sure she always had enough air to breathe. This control made it absolutely clear to her that she's never break free from the grip. She needed a different approach, which meant magic. There wasn't any sun around, so she'd have to use her own reserves. She closed her eyes and gathered her strength.

"They are not your friends. They used their Commanding Voice to make you believe that they are." The voice was quite distracting. "Dragons are evil."

Hurriedly, Nicole thought of a shock wave and pushed the magic out, calling, "Free me!"

She felt the stranger's arms fall away, but the pain in her stomach told her she'd overdone it again. Stumbling two steps forward, she crumpled to the ground. For a moment she stared at the brown leaves, wondering if they were edible, before her world faded and was swallowed by blackness.

I arrived at the castle and slipped in unseen. When no one accosted me, I frowned. Where was Longbow? He'd promised to wait for me near the entrance. As quietly as I could, I hurried through the candle-lit corridor toward my room. As I turned a corner, I bumped into a green dragon. His scales glittered like a mountain of sapphires.

"Why aren't you in your dragon form?" The voice dripped disdain.

"I'm sorry, Mr. Telanuel." The words slipped out before I knew it, but then my thoughts revolted. I had no reason to feel so intimidated. After all, I was the queen-to-be. What right did he have to tell me which body I had to use?

"It's Telanuel. Titles like Mister are for *humans*." He spoke the last word as if he'd said, 'excrement.'

What a snob. With sparkling eyes, I said, "As you please, Telanuel. And to answer your question, I prefer this body at the moment." I walked past him with my head held high. When I was out of sight, I breathed a sigh of relief. Despite the castle's size, it was far too crowded for my taste. Did he live here too? Or had he been visiting the Head of Council? I had to ask Longbow—if I found him.

A little later I stormed into my room. Dinner stood on the table. It was still steaming, which meant Longbow must have brought it recently. My stomach grumbled, but the worry for my servant outweighed my hunger. Deep in my stomach, I knew I had to hurry. A feeling deep inside of me insisted that something bad had happened to him. I turned and left the room. Where now? Left or right? When the urge to hurry grew stronger, I picked a random direction. However, the feeling of something wrong grew stronger too, so I stopped and turned inward.

"Is that you, Mom?"

"Hurry, he's hurt." Mother's voice was full of concern. "You must find him."

"I don't know where to look."

"Remember his scent," Father said. "You're good at that, and then use your nose."

I chided myself for not thinking of this myself and followed Father's advice. Immediately I discovered the scent of pine trees and soap that identified Longbow. Several trails went in and out of my room. I followed the strongest, walking faster and faster. The farther away I got from my living quarters, the stronger the scent became and the darker the corridors.

Soon I was walking downhill in complete darkness. Luckily my eyesight was just as good in the dark as in light. The corridor ended at a massive wooden door, but light spilled through the keyhole. Even with my good sense of smell it was hard to say what lay behind. It smelled of dragons and Longbow but also of decay and age.

I opened the door cautiously. Behind it lay a round room just about big enough for a good-sized dragon. A lonely torch burned in a holder on the wall, illuminating a human body in fetal position in a wet puddle. It took me a moment to realize the black wetness on the floor that sparkled red in the torchlight was blood, and even longer to recognize Longbow, but then I catapulted myself forward to kneel beside him.

"No, no, no, no." I turned Longbow's torso a little sideways to see where the blood was coming from. His fingers cramped around a knife stuck in his belly. I gasped. Who had done this? I couldn't ask him, though, because his eyes stared unseeing past me. At least he was still breathing.

"I need a healer," I said to myself.

"There's no healer stronger than the queen," Mother whispered in my mind.

"If you can't heal him, no one can," Father added.

"But I'm no good at healing." I remembered my failed attempt with Angie. "I'll fail."

"You refused to access Queen's Magic." Was there a tone of disappointment in Mother's voice?

"I don't know how." I stared at the blood seeping past the knife, ending Longbow's life one drop at a time. "No one ever tells me anything about Queen's Magic, only that it's stronger than normal dragon magic."

"Come, fly with us. It will take but a second." Father's golden scales glittered in my peripheral vision. I closed my eyes and found myself flying beside my parents in the whiteness where they seemed to keep existing.

"See this?" Mother pointed with her snout at the whiteness around them. "This is the border between your normal magic and Queen's Magic. Every dragon has their own magic, just like you. And just like you, everyone has their own talents. It is fed by energy you draw from your body or from the nature around you."

"But Queen's Magic is more," Father continued. "It is the collective power, the memories, and the gathered spells of every single royal dragon couple there ever was. All you have to do to access its endless energy is to find your ancestors. And that is something no one can help you with."

"But won't that make me queen automatically?" The thought of getting forced into accepting the role without even the chance of thinking of other options frightened me.

"It only strengthens your claim." Mother's soothing warmth wrapped around me like a wing. "Every child born into this lineage has the right and the ability to access Queen's Magic, but not all will."

"Like your aunt Angie." Father's smile was tangible, like a warm blanket. "She chose not to access her birthright, and she seems happy with the decision."

"But time is running out," Mother urged. "If you want to save your bodyguard, you'll have to find Queen's Magic now." And without further ado, my parents were gone, whipped away by a kind of magic I didn't understand.

"Mom, Dad! Where are you?" But my words echoed through my mind without a reply. I panicked. Flapping my wings, I flew through the white void at top speed without getting anywhere. After all, it wasn't a place. It was my mind. The icy ball in my stomach grew with every heartbeat. I felt more lonely than I'd ever felt before, more lonely than right after Mordekay's murder attempt that had caused my parents' death. It'd been so soothing to know I could still rely on their advice. I whimpered, ready to curl up and die. "Mom! Dad!"

Longbow! I didn't know where the thought had come from, but it reminded me that all could be well still. Hadn't my parents said that I'd have to find my ancestors? They were my ancestors too. Did that mean I'd see them again if I found Queen's Magic? But how did one go about finding magic that wasn't accessible for anyone but members of the royal family?

Stopping mid-flight, I thought—hard—but the only idea I came up with was to use my own magic. Somehow it made sense to search for one kind of magic with the other. Remembering one of my parents' lessons, I tried to believe that magic was like another limb. All I needed to do was figure out how to use this part of myself properly. I swallowed the lump rising in my throat, imagined my magic like an additional arm, stretched it out as far as it would go, and grabbed.

To my surprise, I did feel something in my imaginary hand. It tingled. When I pulled to look at it closer, an unimaginably strong force propelled me toward it. It threatened to break my grip on whatever it was the magic had found. But I wasn't going to give up so easily. With all my might I held on, and it worked.

The white void, although clinging to me with foggy fingers, slowly gave me free. The magic dragged me out of it and into something my mind refused to grasp. Colors whirled around me that I didn't even know a name for. And suddenly my parents were there; not like before when we'd been flying side by side through the white void, but their warmth and joy were unmistakable. And they were not alone. Happy feelings from hundreds of others warmed me, urged me to open my eyes in the real world—and I did.

Although I was still sitting on the ground, cradling Longbow in my arms, the world had changed. Everything sparkled with a multicolored light. With awe I watched strands of magic floating through the room like lazy streams of petals. Only the black hole in the middle of Longbow's belly that greedily swallowed all the threads that swirled through his body terrified me. He breathed so shallow I feared for a moment he was dead already.

Instinctively knowing what needed to be done, I grabbed a couple of green threads and pushed them deep into Longbow's belly. Green for healing. A few cells mended, pushing the tip of the knife up a hair's width. Clearly the magic knew better what needed to be done than I did. I added more and more green until the knife moved out of Longbow's body inch by inch at a steady pace. When it clattered to the ground, I added the other colors; yellow for support, red for love, blue for the water balance in the body, white to tie it all together, and so on. There were many colors to add, and it took me a long while.

I only realized how long when I finally sat up and my muscles complained. Longbow was breathing steadily now, but he'd lost a lot of blood. Hopefully the magic would take care of that problem too. I shivered and looked around once more. The room seemed to be a prison cell, and the walls and ground were slightly damp and very cold. Not the best place for an injured man.

So I turned into my dragon form and shoved a wing under Longbow. It surprised me how strong and flexible it was. I'd never given much thought to the wings, but with it, I managed to get Longbow onto my back. Then I trotted toward my room. I walked slowly so he wouldn't get shaken too badly, for that was probably as bad as the prison's cold dampness.

I found my room without a single wrong turn. Rather proud with myself, I lowered Longbow onto my bed before I turned back into my human form. The delicious smell of my dinner still hung in the air even though the dish was probably barely more than lukewarm. Gosh, how my stomach growled. I pressed both hands onto my belly to suppress the hunger pang. First I needed to make sure that Longbow was okay. I bent over him and noticed his eyelids flicker, so I fetched him a glass of water that I gave him when he sat up. He was so weak I had to support him, but he drank in big gulps.

"I think you're going to be fine now." I sighed with relief. "And about time. I'm starving." I walked over to the table and picked up a fork and the plate.

"No, don't!" He jumped from the bed, clutched his stomach and fell to the ground.

I put plate and fork aside and ran to help him. As I helped him back into my bed—studiously avoiding to worry about what Colin would think about it—I chided him. "You can't get up yet. You nearly died."

"Don't eat that dinner," he said, his skin pale and sweaty. "Please."

"Why?"

"It's got … It's got…" Clearly he couldn't finish his sentence. Beads of sweat rolled down his forehead, as if he was fighting something, so I looked closer. A thin, gray veil seemed to hang over his face. I wiped at it with my magic, but it wouldn't budge. So I used the colorful Queen's Magic without thinking twice about it and ripped the web off.

"Dragon Bane," he said. "It's got Dragon Bane in it."

My jaw dropped and I stared at him, dumbfounded.

Longbow used the break to lie back and breathe. He spoke with his eyes closed. "It's all my fault. I mixed it into your food to poison you."

My mind was reeling and it was impossible to gather my wits for questions.

"You shouldn't have saved me." Tears welled out from under his eyelashes. "I sentenced myself because I'm guilty."

Ridiculous, I thought. He'd been chosen because he was a loyal servant. Someone like him wouldn't go about killing dragons for no reason. And he'd warned me. And anyway, I liked him. There had to be an explanation for his strange behavior.

Maybe there were more magical webs surrounding him. I studied him closer. Bingo! Delicate threads of multicolored magic clung to his throat. Someone had been using Queen's Magic on him. My heart raced as I carefully removed them. Someone who was able to use Queen's Magic meant I had at least one relative the Council didn't know of. Okay, it was someone who tried to kill me and thus probably not the best candidate for becoming queen, but what if there were more? It would mean there was a possible way out. It meant I could live with Colin as a human if only I could find them. The last strand of magic fluttered away, merging happily with the colorful ribbons that now filled my world if I looked closely.

"There were three of them," Longbow whispered. "A small yellow female with rather dull scales. That indicates she hasn't got a hoard. A knight in an armor that bristled with spells and age, and the Native American who used to be Mordekay's servant."

"That was Mordekay. He swapped his body with Blackfeather." I scratched my chin. "I think we need to talk to the others." My stomach grumbled. "But first, we'll have some dinner. Is there a bell to call servants?"

Sixteenth Chapter

When Nicole hadn't found him after fifteen minutes, Harm began to worry. It shouldn't have taken her that long to figure out a simple spell like the tracing spell. What if she'd overdone it again and was now too weak to fetch herself something to eat?

Just when he thought about leaving his hiding place, the knob bumped against his feet. It shone like a small sun. Harm bent down, picked it up, and the glow died. How had the knob found him on its own? And where was Nicole? Something must have happened to her.

He hurried back into the house, but there was no trace of Nicole in her room or the kitchen, and the fridge was untouched. Just in case, he grabbed a carton of orange juice. If she was in need of food, its high sugar content would be a good start.

Then he walked through the house and concentrated on her scent. Every whiff of it made his heart beat faster and his worry bigger. The scent was strongest on the way out. He followed it into the woods, clenching the carton of the orange juice. What if she was unconscious? He couldn't make her drink if she'd used up so much energy. His stomach cramped and sweat broke out. If only he hadn't suggested this stupid experiment. He should have known better. If something bad had happened to her, it was his fault.

Hard-edged stones seemed to push out of his tear ducts, but only normal tears rolled over his cheeks. *That must be what it feels like to cry crystal tears,* Harm thought. He stopped in his tracks and stared into the night without seeing anything but with his mouth wide open in surprise. *Shit. I fell in love with a witch. How did that happen?* He examined his soul and found that a bond had already formed. It was still tender but undeniably there. Oh boy, was he in trouble now. Living in the dragon society, a relationship between a dragon and a human was hard enough. How much harder would it be if the human was a witch? He relaxed a little when he realized that it was unthinkable Nicole would ever see anything more in him than a good friend. But that realization caused even more agony. How could he live without his love fulfilled? For the first time, Harm understood how Blackfeather must have felt after he'd lost his love to Mordekay's magic. He bit his lip, determined not to let his family history repeat itself. He'd have to rip this bond out of his heart somehow, before it got too strong, even if it was the last thing he'd be doing.

But first he had to find Nicole and help her. It wouldn't do to let her down. Sniffing the air, he walked on with renewed determination. Only a few steps later, Nicole's scent mingled with the rusty smell of iron, but without the sweetness that suggested blood. And there was a flowery note too. What had happened here? Had Nicole met someone? He closed his eyes and tried to identify the new scent since it seemed vaguely familiar, but no idea came to him. Who could have known she'd be here? Or had she called someone to pick her up? But the village and its surroundings were shielded from humankind by the strongest spells the dragons were capable of. So who could have breached this defense and why? Just to speak with Nicole? And where did they go then? He began to work in circles around the meeting place, hunting for the scent. Finally, he noticed a trace of the mingled scent moving onward, so he followed it. A few minutes later he arrived at a small clearing, and an all-too-familiar scent drowned out the others.

Blackfeather!

That meant, Nicole had been kidnapped by Mordekay. He had to alert the others. Right away. Wait a moment … Mordekay could no longer turn into a dragon. So how did he get away? Slowly he circled the clearing. He didn't expect a track leading out from it, and his search confirmed his suspicion. Mordekay must have flown off with his dragon ally.

Bad mistake. Harm grinned and walked carefully toward the center of the clearing. *I'll find your scent and then I'll be able to identify you once and for all.* He opened his nostrils as wide as he could, but there was nothing. Not even the scent of Nicole and the iron-flower-person. It was as if someone had cut off all scents at the rim of the clearing. He changed into his dragon form and smelled again, but it didn't make any difference. All he got was a tiny tingle in his nose where Mordekay's scent had met with Nicole's.

He turned back into his human form; it was easier to maneuver between the trees. His shoulders slumped. *If only I'd never suggested this silly training.* But deep down in his heart he knew that it hadn't truly been his fault. Even without the training, Mordekay would have found a different time to kidnap Nicole.

His stomach knotted and he felt tears rise in his eyes, but he fought them down. *I'll find you, Nicole, no matter who took you and where.* With an angry frown on his face, he turned and walked back to the house to tell the others about the kidnapping.

Colin was lying on his bed, daydreaming about being a dragon so he could be with Lydia for good, when his mobile rang. His heart beat a little faster as he accepted the call.

"Hi Colin." Lydia sounded preoccupied or she would have said something like 'sweetiepie" like she usually did, but Colin didn't mind. He loved listening to her voice. "I need you and the others to come to the castle. Something's come up, and we need to talk." Her voice always made him melt inside. How could a voice be this sexy?

"We're on our way," he assured her.

"Love you." She ended the call before he was able to reply. His stomach cramped. Whatever it was she wanted to talk about must have shaken her quite badly, otherwise she wouldn't have missed their usual banter for anything in the world. He jumped off the bed to alert the others.

In the living room, he ran into Harm.

"Nicole's been kidnapped."

Colin's stomach dropped. His sister … his beloved, annoying, six-minutes-younger little sister … gone?

"Who? How? Why?" He didn't seem to be capable of proper speech any longer.

Harm seemed equally agitated. "Mordekay. And the dragon traitor. We were just testing her abilities."

164

It sounded like an excuse to Colin, even though none was necessary. If Mordekay had planned to kidnap Nicole, it would have happened anyway.

"It's not your fault." He pulled out his phone. "Fetch White Crow. I'll tell Lydia."

She answered on the first ring, and he explained. "Hurry over here. It's faster than us coming your way."

"I'll try." She sounded weary. "I'm not sure if I can sneak out. Someone inside the castle has tried to kill my bodyguard and poison me, so they're probably watching."

Colin's stomach knotted. Even imagining something might happen to Lydia had him in a panic. But his sister was missing, so they had to risk it. "Please be careful, honey. I love you so much."

"I'll bring Longbow. Maybe he knows a roundabout way out." She sounded more confident than he felt. "I'll see you in a bit, Sweetiepie."

Colin put away his mobile and shoved both hands through his hair. If only he'd known how dangerous dragon society would be for his love or his sister, he would have done his best to discourage them from coming here. A hand landed on his shoulder.

"We'll find her." Harm's voice held an edge that had never been there before.

Colin turned and saw a devotion in his friend's eyes he knew all too well from his own when he looked into the mirror thinking of Lydia. Harm had fallen for Nicole—could his world become even more complicated? They needed help. Urgently.

"Shouldn't we alert Angie?" There was a tremor in his voice. It would take a while to get Lydia's foster mother here. Did his sister have that much time? Mordekay was bad news and it didn't bode well for Nicole that she had been kidnapped by him. Only his love for Lydia kept the ball of ice in his stomach from freezing him into inaction.

"No. We can handle this." Dressed in soft leather clothes and shoes, White Crow stepped through the door, a bow over the shoulder, a spear in one hand, and a silver-tipped lance in the other that he handed to Harm. "Ready. Show me the place."

"I could use the tracking spell I tried to teach Nicole." Harm's right hand tightened around the spear's shaft until his knuckles turned white.

"You said they flew away. So how big is the spell's circle of influence? And do you have the necessary peace of mind for spellcasting?" White Crow looked Harm in the eyes. Colin shivered even though the gaze wasn't aimed at him.

Wordlessly Harm turned and took the lead. The three only walked a few minutes to reach a clearing barely big enough for one dragon to land. White Crow asked them to wait at its perimeter. Then he rounded the clearing in ever-tightening circles, bent over far enough that his nose was at knee-level. Every so often he picked something up, sniffed or tasted, shook his head and moved on. In the end he even climbed a few trees. When he returned, a dragon-shaped shadow appeared in the circle of sky visible above the clearing.

Colin recognized it immediately. "Lydia! Down here."

She landed, and Colin ran to her, followed by Harm and White Crow. In silence they helped a young Native American from her back who seemed weak as a baby but otherwise unhurt.

"Let's get him somewhere warm." Lydia's voice sounded worried. "And then bring me up to date."

"I'm not going to sit around chatting while Nicole needs me." Harm balled his hands into fists. Heat radiated from him and Colin took a step back, just in case. He knew all too well how easily the dragon's temper could flare up.

"It is clear that Mordekay has at least one if not more allies." Lydia looked Harm straight in the eye. "And they're set on destroying not only me but everyone I care about. You won't be able to help Nicole if you don't know which precautions to take."

After a staring contest of maybe ten seconds, Harm lowered his gaze. "You're right." With hanging shoulders he followed her. Colin helped White Crow to support Lydia's bodyguard.

When they'd finally set Longbow down on the sofa, White Crow reported his finds.

"There were clear traces of two people: a female I took for Nicole, and an ambiguous in cheap black clothes. The only disturbing fact about that is this." He held out a vicious-looking knife. "It's a dragon slayer's knife. See the little bottle here?" He pointed to a glass vial set into the ivory hilt. "It contains Dragon Bane. The smallest wound caused by this knife would be deadly for any dragon. What irritates me is that there haven't been any dragon slayers since the dragons left Europe."

"I was attacked by a knight on the way here," Lydia said. "Might that have been the dragon slayer?"

"It could well be. It's hard to say." White Crow stuck the dagger into his belt. "Beside the two humans, I found traces of at least two dragons, one of them white."

"White?" Lydia's head snapped up. "But I thought Mom and I were the only white dragons."

"White isn't such a rare color," Harm said. "The whole family of the Chinese queen is white."

"It is a royal color. No other dragon has it." White Crow sat in a chair beside the sofa and folded his left leg over his right.

"So we'll have to assume they've got someone who can access Queen's Magic."

"That makes sense," Longbow said. "I've been Commanded, and that had me troubled the whole time. For all my life, I've trained to ignore the Commanding Voice. I just couldn't explain why I wasn't able to shake it this time."

Colin frowned. He didn't understand.

Luckily Lydia noticed his confusion. "The Commanding Voice of a potential queen is much, much stronger than the normal one."

"Naturally there is also a magical way to enhance a Commanding Voice," White Crow said. "We can't rule out the possibility that the white scales I found have been harvested from Lydia and planted as a ruse for us."

"But it is also possible that a dragon from a royal dragon family exists and helps Mordekay, right?" An idea occurred to Colin that seemed to turn the blood in his veins into ice. "Could it be used to Compel a big group of humans?"

"I don't know, but I think it might be possible," White Crow said. "Why? Do you think the other potential queen will use it on us so Mordekay can get at Lydia more easily?"

"Worse." Colin felt the blood drain from his face but couldn't prevent it. "Just imagine Mordekay gets his potential queen to Command our president. It could result in the military hunting down all dragons. Or worse, Mordekay might end up controlling the fate of all humans in the US."

The room fell silent, and Colin watched as the faces around him paled significantly.

Lydia was the first to speak again. "But what would he need Nicole for?"

"She's a witch." Harm's face was drawn. "There are lots of things a dragon can do with a witch … or with her blood."

Again they fell silent until White Crow got up. "I see that we have to find Nicole right now. I will get Herbert to help me search the mountains. Colin and Harm, you should travel through the forest in human guise. Maybe the dragons landed early. Try to find them, but don't attack them without calling us." He turned to Lydia. "Go back to the castle and read the scrolls and books in your library and draw a genealogical tree. We need to know where this potential queen comes from if there really is one."

"But I can't read the script. It's all foreign." Lydia's eyes were wide as if in a panic. Instinctively Colin put his arm around her shoulders.

White Crow smiled at them. "Your parents can teach you. Believe me, for a queen it's so much easier than for anyone else. And anyway, as a toddler, you were already able to read dragon script. It's just a question of rediscovering a known skill."

Lydia nodded and turned to go. Then she stopped and turned back. "You know what I just thought?" She continued without waiting for an answer. "The knight knew exactly when and where to attack me when I came here, but the only person we told was the Head of Council so she could arrange for someone to pick me up."

Colin saw right away where her thought was leading. "That narrows the suspects. The traitor must have been someone who knew about your change of plans."

"I'll need to talk to the Head of Council." Lydia didn't sound particularly fond of the idea. "I need to know who she told."

"She told everybody around dinner time the day of your arrival," Longbow said. "She wanted a decent reception for you."

"By that time I was already airborne." Lydia nodded to him and sighed. "I'll talk to her."

A few minutes later, Lydia and White Crow had left. Colin looked at Longbow. "Will you be alright when we're gone?"

"All I need is some rest, and I'm pretty sure I'll get it here." The young man smiled but his eyes remained stern. "You go and find the witch-girl."

Colin did his best to force his nearly frozen body to follow Harm. Everything inside screamed at him to follow Lydia and help her, but that would mean failing his sister. *Lydia can take care of herself. Trust her. She's a strong dragon,* he reassured himself, but the whole time he followed Harm through the dark forest he couldn't shake the feeling of dread that had crept into his heart.

SEVENTEENTH CHAPTER

*W*hen Nicole woke, she was lying on packed earth with a thin layer of straw. Her arms were tied behind her back, and it was dark. Only a small glimmer of light fell through the wooden wall in front of her nose. She must be in a barn or in a stable. Who would have thought that something like this existed in dragon country?

There were people talking at a slight distance. Maybe she could alert them to her presence. A young female voice complained about having missed dinner, and a much too familiar voice cut her off.

"Stop whining," Mordekay said.

Nicole flinched. If he got her again, she was in bad trouble.

Mordekay went on. "Better tell me where the knight is. He should have been here an hour ago."

The young-sounding girl answered so low that Nicole couldn't understand her. Wriggling as best she could, she tried to get closer to the wall so she could peek through a gap in the wood. If the two were alone, all she had to do was get rid of her bonds and flee. She tried to rip the cord, but the knot was well bound and the fibers too new. She swore silently until she remembered that she was a witch now. She was already planning a new spell that'd dissolve the cord when she remembered how she'd knocked herself out the last time she'd tried magic. Maybe she wasn't meant to use it after all … at least not without proper tutoring. With a sigh she gave up her struggles for the moment and concentrated on the voices.

"Why do we need a knight anyway?" the girl wanted to know. "He gives me the creeps. Do you know he's got a knife with a Dragon Bane vial in it?"

"He's a dragon slayer, for crying out loud. Don't you have any brain in that head of yours?" Mordekay seemed to be his usual cheery self.

"I still don't like him." It sounded as if the girl was pouting, since the two stopped talking.

"I'm not going to explain why we need him. Not again." Mordekay obviously had started pacing because the sounds of feet on straw accompanied his words. "Where in the Dragon Mother's name are they?" He didn't get an answer, but this time he hadn't sounded as if he'd expected one.

The whoosh of dragon's wings alerted Nicole to a change.

A little later, a new voice greeted Mordekay.

"What took you so long?" The former black dragon was clearly annoyed.

"He had to bring a generator, and it took a while to find one that wasn't too heavy for me." The newcomer greeted the girl but she didn't answer him either, so he turned back to Mordekay. "It seems that with such a small generator, the power of the output will be rather limited. But I'm no scientist. Let the knight explain, he's better at it."

"I'm better at what?" The voice sounded just as young as the girl. Could that be the knight? In Nicole's mind, a knight was bearded and at least of middle age with lots of battle scars. But now that she thought about it, hadn't Sir Galahad from the legend of King Arthur been rather young? Obviously they must start becoming a knight at some point. She wriggled even closer to the gap in the wall, but there wasn't much to see; only the tail of a white robe and black boots.

"With all that electrical stuff," the other man said. "I don't understand half of it."

"I think you're doing fine." The knight set something down that rattled a lot. "You've learned how to use my little baby." Flesh slapped metal. "All this needs to run is a generator and the little program I wrote."

"We've got a generator," Mordekay said. "Now hand over the program."

"All in good time." The knight seemed more wary than Nicole had expected. "Can I have something to eat now? I'm starving."

Soon, slurping and chewing noises replaced the words.

Nicole searched her mind feverishly for something, anything, even a spell that would help her get away from these lunatics. But the only spell she remembered was the tracer spell Harm had shown her before she was kidnapped. What if she adapted it a little? If she could make an item find Harm, maybe by rolling or flying over the ground, he'd surely come and rescue her. She rolled a little more onto her back so her fingers could search the ground. When they closed around a pebble, she shut her eyes and recalled Harm's face. Immediately she began to relax. She felt calm and protected. Harm would come and get her. All she needed to do was get the pebble to fetch him. She spoke to the small stone as if it was alive, but only in her mind. She didn't want her captors to know she had woken.

"I need you to be brave, little stone. Find Harm and bring him here. Please. You're my only hope." As she talked, the stone seemed to warm up. When she couldn't think of anything else to say, she spoke the activation word Harm had taught her. "Mechadjidj."

The pebble wriggled in her hands until she let it go. Glowing softly, it rolled past her face to the gap in the wooden wall and squeezed through. Nicole helped it along with her nose when it threatened to get stuck. Then she leaned back, hoped the dragons wouldn't see the stone's faint glow, and waited. Her stomach grumbled.

"Say, when are you going to let the witch go?" The knight was speaking with his mouth full, but Nicole understood him anyway.

"Why would I do that?" Mordekay seemed surprised. "After all the trouble we had to get her."

"We need her," the young female said. "Don't you know that a witch's blood is the best source for magical power? We can do spells with it that are impossible to break, even for a queen. And the dragons don't even have a queen yet."

Nicole's stomach dropped as if she were sitting in a roller coaster. The wanted to use her blood? How much of it? Would she survive? *Please, Harm, come real fast.*

"That's horrific. You can't just go and steal a human's blood." The knight's voice rose. "And it's against our agreement. I said I'd help you against the dragons if you paid my price, but humans have never been part of the deal."

"She's a witch, idiot. Stop thinking of her!" There was an undertone in the girl's voice that made the hairs on Nicole's arms stand up. Was she using magic on the knight? Whatever it was, it didn't seem to work.

"You can't order me around," the knight said. "And I'll most definitely not help you to kill a human, for even a witch is human." A spoon clanked against a metal pot or plate. "I'm a free man, so I'll leave now, and I'll take the witch with me."

"Sorry, but I won't let you." Mordekay's voice was dangerously low and followed by a thud, a muffled cry of pain and another thud. Nicole pressed her eye to the gap in the wall, but all she could see were feet. Someone was lying on the ground. When the feet started moving in her direction, she rolled back into the position she had been in before, closed her eyes, and pretended to be unconscious still.

Things—or a person?—were dragged over the ground, people grunted and swore, doors opened and clanked shut, and someone was dumped right beside her.

"What are we going to do with him?" The girl's voice came from somewhere near Nicole's feet.

"The less you know the better." Mordekay's voice was so close that he must have been the one to drag the body. Cloth rustled as he searched the knight's pockets. For a moment Nicole worried that the young man was dead already, but when Mordekay swore, she remembered that they were missing a program for whatever gadget the knight had built for them.

The stranger's voice whispered, "His aunt will never hand over the program for the gadget if he isn't there."

"I know." Mordekay's steps retreated to where Nicole had heard the girl. "We'll keep him for a while longer, but as soon as I have my body back, it'll be my greatest pleasure to eat him."

More shuffling and the door closed behind them. Nicole breathed out, only noticing now that she'd held her breath.

When she was sure that her captors had returned to their meal, she sat up and looked over to the figure sprawled on the ground beside her. The knight wore black jeans, a black leather jacket, and a black T-shirt, and … he was, without a question, a girl.

I landed, turned into my human form as fast as I could, and walked swiftly toward the entrance. I was secretly annoyed that I had to do research while Colin and Harm went looking for Nicole. She was my friend too. To ease my worries, I repeated the reasons we needed to know what only I could find out. We might be facing a magic user, a dragon, with the strength of Queen's Magic, and it would be best to know who that dragon was. And to get out of becoming queen, I needed a replacement. This information was hidden in the dragons' library, and only I could learn the script fast enough. Still, I felt as if I was abandoning Nicole.

I was just approaching the staircase in the great hall when a huge green dragon shot through the entrance and nearly landed on top of me. I jumped aside at the last possible moment.

"Telanuel!" My voice held more anger than I'd meant to use.

"I'm sorry, Your Majesty. I didn't expect anyone to be here." To my surprise, Telanuel turned into his human form. Even as a bearded man, he towered over me until he bowed deeply. The gesture, although customary, made me feel uncomfortable.

"Please, don't." I grabbed his shoulder and pulled him up again. An idea occurred to me. "Telanuel, do you know how the library is organized?" He might not like me much, but he was working for the Head of Council. He should be obliged to help me.

"Naturally." He stood straight. "Is there anything in particular you're interested in?" He started walking in the direction of the library. "And, if I may inquire as to the whereabouts of your bodyguard? He should be able to help you with the library."

I held my breath for a moment. What did he know about my bodyguard? But then I remembered that he worked for the Head of Council. She surely had told him about Longbow. Now the question remained of how much I could trust him. Surely he would report to the Head of Council, and I didn't know how good that would be. So I kept the facts to a minimum. "He brought me my dinner and left. I haven't seen him since."

"Hmm. I assigned him to you myself and his order was to stay close to you at all times." He sounded irritated. "I'll have to look into that. So, did you like your dinner?"

"I didn't eat it." I remained cautious, but had to give a reason that would explain why I didn't eat the meal Longbow had brought. The dragons would soon find out that I was still alive, and the traitor would wonder. With a good explanation he'd not realize that I noticed the poison. Hopefully Telanuel would spread the word. "I wasn't hungry. All the excitement, you know?"

"Oh yes, the Head of Council said you'd adapted to human ways. I'm sorry." He held open the small door inside the bigger portal leading into the library, and I wasn't sure if he was sorry for my preference of humans or for Longbow bringing me my dinner. He didn't give me time to wonder about that. "So, what exactly are you looking for?"

"I'd like to learn more about my ancestry." Researching my family was something that should please the dragons, so I gave the information without hesitation, pushing the niggling thought that I was running out of time to the back of my mind. "It might be nice to know that I'm not truly alone."

A smile warmed his stern face. It was such an unusual expression that I took a step back. "But as a queen-to-be you shouldn't feel lonely. If you access Queen's Magic, there shouldn't be a need for you to read about your ancestors."

"What do you mean?" I pretended not to understand. After all, it was none of his business whether I felt my parents nearby or not. "How can I know my relatives by using a different kind of magic?"

"I'll leave it to the Head of Council to explain. She's more knowledgeable about such matters." He bowed with a flourish. "Please come this way. We've got a scroll with your whole lineage."

I wondered about his strange behavior but followed him deeper into the library. He led me to a huge table with a scroll on spindles attached to both sides. He rolled the scroll completely onto the right-hand spindle, unhooking it from the left hand one, lifted it from its holder, and told me to wait. While I teetered on the balls of my feet, he walked off and returned with a different scroll that he set into the free holder. Then he pulled the loose end all the way over the table and hooked some tiny little eyelets into the hooks on the left-hand spindle. Then he turned a lever on the left-hand spindle. I looked at the scroll where the neat, strange writing of draconian script moved past me at the speed with which he turned the lever. Once in a while he pointed out some important items.

"That branch there is the Chinese one, and that one down here is the European branch of your family. You can see there that none of them remained in the old country; they all emigrated here. If you keep going there's a branch from the African and the South American dragons too, because they married into your family two or three generations back. If you go all the way to the right, you'll find your parents, your deceased siblings and yourself. As soon as you ascend the throne, your name will get gilded." He bowed once more. "I'll leave you to it now, but I'll be back to put the scroll away. I'll also make sure that Longbow gets a reprimand for his long absence."

"Thank you," I said, knowing full well that he wouldn't be able to find Longbow.

I waited until I heard the door click closed behind him before I turned my attention to the script. Despair crept into my heart as I stared at the illegible scribbles. I'd never learn to read this in the little time I had. Everything inside of me screamed to drop this research and start searching for Nicole.

But then warmth enveloped me, and I remembered my parents in the realm of Queen's Magic. Maybe they could help me. I concentrated on finding that realm, and it was right there. I slipped into it as if I'd never done anything else in my life. Of course my parents waited for me, together with every other dragon on this scroll that wasn't alive any longer.

I turned the levers and scrolled through the long line of ancestors, family side lines, and died-out threads, and every dragon in my mind, or wherever else Queen's Magic was, read his or her name. The longer I listened, the more the scratchy letters made sense. By the time my parents whispered their names, I could read them easily. Wow, that was the best and easiest way to learn ever. If only that would work with the stuff I needed to understand for school too. I sighed, knowing I'd never make a really good full-time human. It felt as if life itself was trying to force me to become the next dragon queen, but I wouldn't give up my dream of living with Colin.

Eighteenth Chapter

"You're straying, Lydia," Father said. "Time is running out, and you need to concentrate."

I pulled my thoughts back to the scroll. Of course. The others would be waiting, hopefully with news about Nicole. I started reading the scroll backwards, starting with my parents. Mother's siblings all died without children, aside from Angie. But she didn't have any children either, so that was a dead end. I went back another generation, and another one. My great-grandmother married a Chinese prince. Well, that might be a thread with potential candidates. I followed the marriages of my great-grandfather's siblings, but only one made it to adulthood. Her name was gilded, so I took it for granted that she'd become the Chinese queen.

"That is correct," Mother confirmed. "Hurry, honey. We need to get going."

I read on. The Chinese line remained thin. Again, only one of the children made it to adulthood, and she died soon after she laid her first clutch of eggs. Until the coronation of the eldest of the only two dragonets of that clan, their father must have taken on the queen's duties since his name was silver-plated. To my surprise, the next queen was the younger one of the two surviving siblings. "What happened to the older one?" I turned inward and looked at my great-grandfather, a stately midnight blue dragon.

"She got lost in a snowstorm and died far from home." A tear rolled down his cheek, hissing gently.

"Her soul never found her way here," my great-grandmother added. Her white scales dimmed as she spoke. "She did have a daughter, and there must be a grandchild, whether female or male we do not know."

"But there are no names on the scroll." I pointed to the relevant section.

"The scroll's magic only gets the names of those children named by their parents." Mother smiled at me, obviously willing me to understand something.

"But how do you know the child is still alive?" No one answered my question and I realized why, when I remembered the attack on Longbow. Someone had ordered him to kill himself despite the fact that he'd trained to withstand the Commanding Voice. "The grandchild taps into Queen's Magic!"

"Yes, but it does so in a rather strange way." My grandmother shook her wings and little eddies of love danced around me. "Normally, only a girl should be capable of yielding Queen's Magic, but this use is so unusual that we can't tell whether it's a boy or a girl. Also, we can only guess at the age. The child must be slightly older than you are."

"And since neither name shows up on this scroll, they must both have gotten their names from someone else. That means they've both been foster children." I turned the right-hand lever as fast as I could to roll up the scroll. "I'd love to know the reason, she's working for Mordekay." When I got to the end, I unhooked the scroll, but I left it in the holder—after all, I didn't know where it belonged—and hurried out of the library and through the corridors. I needed to call Colin, and my mobile got no connection this deep inside a mountain. Come to think of it, it was surprising that the mobiles worked at all this far away from human civilization.

"We're not living behind the moon," Mother said, and I felt her smile.

"Your grandparents had electricity installed, and we added mobile phone masts, landlines, cable TV, and broadband Internet." Father's voice sounded smug. "But none of that is relevant now. We believe your second cousin is hiding in a cave, and I fear your friends are getting too close to her. Without your help they don't stand a chance."

Of course, my worry and the sense of urgency increased. Why did he have to tell me? I couldn't run faster than I already was.

I had barely reached the entrance hall when my mobile beeped. Colin had messaged me.

Found a trail, will write soon oxo

I was just about to turn into my dragon form when Telanuel's big green body blocked the entrance.

"I'm truly sorry to interrupt you, but the Chinese Head of Council wants to talk to you."

"The Chinese?" My head whirled. Had they found out about their missing princess too? Would they come and fetch her? Would she be welcome? And how deeply was she involved in Mordekay's schemes? "Do I have to come?"

"You're the queen-to-be. It's your duty." Telanuel's face was as stern as ever.

"But my friends need me." The tug of urgency I felt in my bones like a fishing line pulling me in the direction of my friends increased even more. In my worry, I said more than I'd meant to say. "They're hunting Mordekay."

Telanuel's face darkened. As a fleeting surprise I acknowledged the fact that I was obviously able to read dragon expressions. He actually frowned, something that wasn't easy to achieve with so many ridges and horns on one's face. "They should have left that to me. I'm the Queen's and the Council's Head of Security. Let's take care of the Chinese first and then go and help your friends. I'll come along."

Thankful for his immediate support without questions, I nodded and turned into my dragon form to follow him to the throne room. I still felt as if someone was ripping my heart out.

Harm scolded himself for the umpteenth time that he hadn't used the tracking spell at a time when there was still a chance Nicole was in its sphere of influence. Now he had to stomp blindly through the forest, hoping for a trace of Nicole's scent. He opened his nostrils as wide as he could and sucked in the night air.

Wait a moment. There was something … something was coming their way. Something small and smelling of Nicole.

"I texted Lydia that we've found a clue." Colin said. "I know it's not really true, but…"

"Shhh." Harm held up a hand. He strained into the darkness of the forest, but nothing could be heard. Even the small creatures' rustling seemed to have stopped. How could whatever was coming be so silent? He strained his eyes to see, but the light of the moon wasn't bright enough to illuminate the forest floor properly.

Something bumped against the back of his foot. He had to crouch to make out that it was a small, glowing pebble. It was moving of its own accord and smelled very strongly of Nicole. *She used the spell again,* he thought, and pride filled his heart. His little witch was making big progress even under duress. He turned to Colin and pointed at the stone.

"Here's our clue." He picked it up and held it on the palm of his hand, allowing Colin to scrutinize it. Although the stone had found him, the light didn't die. More, the little stone kept rolling northward. Was the spell still active? Had Nicole adapted it somehow?

"It's magical." Colin sounded surprised.

"You sister put a spell on it." Harm realized that she must have modified the one he had taught her. Heat surged through his veins. Wow, what a witch she was turning out to be.

The stone rolled around on his palm, pointing north, more insistent with every second.

"What are we waiting for?" Colin took a step in the direction it indicated.

"We should alert White Crow." Although Harm, too, felt like storming off, he knew they shouldn't try to take on Mordekay and his allies on his own.

"He has no mobile, and we're losing time if we turn back to find him." Colin set out northward. "And anyway, who knows how long her spell will last?"

Those were excellent arguments there. Wordlessly, Harm broke a branch on the nearest tree without ripping it off—the easiest way to mark the way for White Crow—and marched north.

Half an hour and many broken branches later, Harm and Colin emerged from the forest. Not far from them a low, wooden building with a shingled roof stood in the moonlight. Behind it, the mountain rose higher and higher. The stone strained in the direction of the building.

"It's a barn." Colin's voice sounded surprised.

"It's for the cattle in summer when some of the herd is grazing here." Harm crouched to show a smaller silhouette. "It looks deserted, but the stone is hopping, so I think that might be their hiding place."

Colin crouched beside them. As close to the ground as possible without lying down, they moved toward the barn. When they reached the southernmost corner, Harm peeked around to the east side to the front entrance.

"The doors are wide open. It looks like they've left." He got up. His disappointment was so strong he struggled to stand. "We're too late."

"Hmmmblmmm." The strange sound came from the barn's backside. Harm looked at Colin, who stared back wide-eyed. They held their breath.

"Hmmmblmmm." The sound repeated, followed by a splashing noise.

"The trough." Harm ran. As he'd thought, someone was lying in the watering trough behind the barn, face already under water. Harm grabbed the person and pulled, only to notice that the trough's draining hole had been plugged. Water ran off the human who coughed and spat and wriggled to break free. A wave of scent filled the air. It was familiar, very familiar, but it wasn't Nicole's. A giant fist squeezed Harm's chest.

"Luke. What are you doing here?" Harm shook his classmate, not too hard but insistently.

"Luke?" Colin peered around Harm. "But that's a girl."

"I'm … not … a … girl." Luke fought for air. Coughing and gasping shook his body. "I'm a … knight."

"*You're* the knight?" Anger erupted in Harm like a volcano and it took all of his strength not to strangle the girl.

"You tried to kill Lydia!" Colin seemed just as angry as he was. Suddenly Harm was glad for the company.

"She's their queen. Dragons are helpless without their queen. You should be glad I'm here to protect you from the evil brood." Still dripping but breathing normally again, Luke turned and lifted his hands that were tied on his back. "Can you please untie me?"

Harm balled his hands into fists, unable to speak.

"She's not queen yet, and she doesn't *want* to be queen." Colin folded his arms in front of his chest. "And for all we know, you're in cohorts with Mordekay."

"At least that man knows there's a need for knights." Luke didn't turn back around. He simply stood there waiting to be untied. "He even caught a female. I just don't understand why he pampers her so much."

Suddenly all the anger left Harm. It evaporated like a dewdrop in the sun. His shoulders slumped and he put a hand on Colin's arm. "It's not Luke's fault that she doesn't understand. Mordekay has a way with people. They simply trust him. And knights have always been afraid of us."

"Us?" Luke shot around, eyes wide and looking scared.

"Mordekay is a dragon, as am I." Harm shrugged, and flickered, something he hadn't done since he'd been a fledgling. The rapid shifting of body parts blurred into the visual image of his dragon shape overlaying a human body. It was quite an impressive show that fledglings enjoyed, but nothing a grown dragon would resort to. Still, Harm thought it best to impress Luke, and it seemed to work. The girl-knight stared wordlessly at him with her mouth hanging wide open.

"You know," Harm said as he turned her around and untied her hands. "You should learn how to identify dragons before you go blundering in, killing dragons left and right. Haven't the other knights taught you anything?"

To his surprise, Luke's knees buckled and she sank to the ground the minute the rope fell away. She put her hands over her face and began to cry. Harm crouched beside her and put his arm around her shoulder. "What's wrong?"

Luke cried, hiccupped, and cried some more.

"What about your parents?" Colin asked, and the anger in his voice was still palpable. "Do they know what you're up to? Or are they knights too?"

It took a while before Luke was able to answer. "I'm the last one. The last knight. My parents are dead, murdered by a gigantic black dragon. That's when I swore to rid the world of the evil dragons."

"That was surely Mordekay." Colin sat down on a big rock beside the water trough. "At least, he is a big, black dragon if he's in his normal body."

"He's not?" Luke looked up and her face was pale as ashes.

"Nope. He's in the body of Harm's biological father right now who's in Mordekay's true body." Colin shrugged. "It's complicated."

"Mordekay is planning on murdering a black dragon to take over his body." Luke's voice wobbled. "God, I got it all wrong. It's all my fault." She started crying again.

Harm grabbed her face with both hands and forced her to look up. "It's not your fault. Mordekay is probably the only dragon capable of lying, or he's extremely good at twisting the truth. The only error you made is trusting him. Everything else is his fault. Now, tell me where he took Nicole."

If possible, Luke grew even paler. "The witch?"

"My sister!" Colin sat, arms akimbo. "My twin sister."

Luke's answer was barely audible. "He needs her blood to take over the dragon's body."

"Okay, that's it." Colin got up. "We've wasted enough time. Let's go and bring Mordekay to justice."

Harm's heart pumped hard in his chest and red veils drifted through his vision when he thought about Mordekay killing Nicole. Still, there was the issue of the female dragon who was working with him, and whomever else he'd recruited. Sure, he was as angry and as determined to get Nicole back alive as Colin was, but he also knew that they didn't stand a chance on their own. "We need White Crow and Herbert."

"Why do you need us?" White Crow stepped from the shadows of the barn, and Harm shot around. Gosh, that man could move quietly. White Crow whistled, and a dragon landed right beside them. In the moonlight he looked rather small, and his scales were pink.

"Herbert." Harm breathed a sigh of relief before launching into a shortened version of what they'd just found out. Meanwhile, Herbert sniffed the ground around the barn.

"She was here not an hour ago," he confirmed when Harm was done. "Her track leads toward the mountains, and they must have walked. It seems they weren't worried about being discovered."

"Where do you think they're headed?" White Crow climbed onto Herbert's back, and the pink dragon started walking.

188

"Probably one of the caves up there." He lifted his muzzle toward the mountain behind the barn.

Harm and Colin followed them, and with every step Nicole's scent grew stronger. A huge wave of relief washed through Harm. She'd been alive about an hour ago. Strangely enough the thought fired up his anger even more. "I'll fly ahead," he announced and turned.

"Take me along," Colin said, and Harm waited until his friend had climbed onto his back before he took off. When he had reached a good height for flying, he glanced back down. Luke was trudging after Herbert and White Crow, a sword in one hand and a lance in the other.

Nineteenth Chapter

*N*icole's feet hurt and her stomach grumbled, probably from using her magic on the pebble, when they finally reached a cave entrance just about big enough to admit the long, snake-like body of the white dragon that was traveling with them. Nicole had to stoop to follow her into a cave much bigger than she'd anticipated. What surprised her even more were the mid-sized red dragon and the gigantic back one lying on the ground beside an open fire. According to Harm's explanations, the black dragon had to be Blackfeather. Could the red one be Angie? And how did they get in here? It dawned on her when she spotted the chains attached to the wall with one end and to the shackles on the dragons' limbs with the other. The white dragon must have ordered them to turn into humans and back.

Well, that was one secret solved. Now for a way to flee. Mordekay was busy setting up a big, foldable, gilded table, but the white dragon blocked the entrance, so Nicole looked around for a different way out, but the small entrance seemed the only place to leave the spacious cave. Nicole frowned. Considering the size of the cave and the comparatively small entrance, it should have been much darker, but the walls glowed with a soothing bluish light.

"Stop gawking." Mordekay grabbed her arm and pushed her into an iron cage that stood in a corner, looking like a prop from a medieval festival. But he secured it with a brand new padlock and went back to whatever he was preparing. Drat. How could she escape stuck in a cage? The bars were sturdy despite the rust.

The white dragon settled beside her and stared at her with big, green eyes. "Are you really a witch?"

"Are you really working with Mordekay?"

"He's a good guy." The white dragon narrowed her eyes. "He never ridiculed me for my deformation."

What was the dragon talking about? She was as perfect a Chinese dragon as Nicole had ever seen, just much more alive than the paper mâché versions during Chinese New Year. Before she could say so, Mordekay came over and shooed the white dragon away.

"The red dragon is waking. Tell it again to sleep." He crouched in front of Nicole. "Now, my little sweetheart. Let's establish one thing. I do not like my plans to get crossed; especially not by a bunch of children and fledglings. And I will show your friends just what it means to mess with me." He pointed to the black dragon. "With my own body this close, I can access more magic than you'll ever be able to use, puny human. You will obey every single word I say!"

There was a strange vibration in the words that made them seem larger, more powerful. Nicole's arms and legs suddenly felt tied with invisible tendrils, and her head nodded without her consent. Was that the Commanding Voice Lydia had insisted Mordekay had used on her before? But why didn't she feel like last time? As far as she remembered, she'd been more or less out of her mind when Mordekay used it on her. Even now she could only recall bits and pieces of that night. However, right now, her mind was as clear as ever. She was still master of her own thoughts.

Mordekay opened the cage door. "Now, come along to the stone table over there."

Her body obeyed and walked through the cave, but Nicole managed to slow it down considerably even when Mordekay told her to hurry.

"Lie down." The magic dripped from his voice, and Nicole obeyed again. When she felt the smooth coldness in her back, she realized that she could get up and leave now. The strings of the Commanding Voice were gone. Had her own magic canceled Mordekay's influence on her? Or was she simply becoming immune against his commands?

"Remain here and don't move." The new command fixed her body to the stone slab better than any chain would have done. She snorted angrily. Then an idea occurred to her. Would he tell her how long she was to stay? Maybe the new command would wear off if she lay there for just a while. She had to give her magic some time to figure out the loopholes.

The white dragon inched closer and nudged her. "I've never seen a witch before," it whispered.

Nicole's thoughts immediately focused on the Chinese dragon. With Mordekay busy lifting the black dragon's head and pulling it along inch by inch, the sinuous female was the only one in the way of her flight. She felt the ties of Mordekay's command wearing thin already. A few more minutes and she'd be able to leave. She had to distract the dragon and, if possible, get it to fall asleep or some such.

"Can you do some magic?" The white dragon's voice sounded eager. "Just something small to show me."

"No," Nicole said. "It would drain my energy too much. How come you think you're deformed?"

The dragon's eyes opened wide. "Can't you see how skinny and long I am? No dragon I've seen looks like that. I'm uglier than anyone."

"I think you're beautiful." Nicole was just about to tell the dragon that she looked just like all Chinese dragons—at least, Nicole suspected that all Chinese dragons looked like this one—when Mordekay snapped at her. "Stop talking to her."

Nicole's jaws and lips moved but no sound came out. She shrugged apologetically at the white dragon, who frowned at Mordekay.

"You didn't need to do that." She sounded petulant like a small child. "I just wanted someone to talk to. I didn't tell her any of our secrets."

"What would be the use of that?" Mordekay's voice sounded strained. Obviously pulling the black dragon was much more exhausting than he had anticipated, even though he was using magic, as Nicole felt. He lifted the heavy head and placed it on the golden table right beside her. "The witch will be dead before the hour is out."

Nicole's hands and feet grew cold. She felt around for the invisible threads, but they were gone except for the ones closing her mouth.

The white dragon slunk away to a corner of the cave, curled up with her back to Mordekay and sulked. And Mordekay was busy shifting the black dragon's head into a better position on the slightly wobbly table. There wouldn't be a better time to flee.

Just as Nicole inched sideways to slip off the table, something small and cold bumped against her hand. What was that? The nose of an animal? She blinked and glanced to her hand. Her pebble! It had returned. She held her breath and listened intently. Did that mean Harm was here too? Her heart fluttered. With Harm's help, she would surely be able to flee. He was so much stronger than the Chinese girl.

With Telanuel's big, green body at my side, I entered the throne room in my dragon form and every dragon in sight lowered its head. Immediately my heart began to thump heavily. I hurried toward the front where the Head of Council was awaiting me, flipping her tail to and fro impatiently.

"Hurry up," she hissed. "They're waiting." She pointed to a glassy-looking bubble hovering in the air in front of the throne. An official-looking Chinese dragon, dark blue with silver beard, mane, and fronds, frowned at them out of the bubble. *The glass must be some kind of communicating device,* I thought as I stepped beside the head of Council and bowed.

"I am honored to—"

"Thank you for finally showing up, Your Majesty," the Chinese dragon interrupted me, something I'd thought impossible considering the Chinese's ultimate need for politeness. Were Chinese dragons different from the country's humans? I opened my mouth to ask what the ambassador wanted, when he continued without waiting for my question. "I am acutely aware that you are new to your responsibilities and might not even know that the Head of Council sent a servant to our queen not one moon ago. It was received with due gratitude and treated well. Still, it commenced to murder our beloved queen, her husband, and all of their children last night. We're still in shock."

I understood perfectly. Their shock reverberated through my bones as if someone had rung a big gong. I shivered, but then something occurred to me.

"Did he use Dragon's Bane?" The scenario sounded too familiar to be a coincidence. The Chinese dragon's nod confirmed my suspicion, so I said, "I'd like to talk to him."

"That is not possible since our Head of Security ate it." The blue dragon shook his mane. "Our investigation clearly shows that he'd been ordered to kill, and therefore our nation now considers itself at war with your nation. As soon as the traditional Time of Mourning is over, we will wipe you and your human servants off the planet." Before I could stop him, he bowed stiffly and the glass emptied.

I stopped my protest before it left my mouth. It wouldn't do to alert the gathered dragons to the fact that there was at least one traitor in their midst. Turning to the Head of Council, I asked, "Why did you sent that servant?"

"It was Queen Sun Shin's seventieth coronation anniversary." The Head of Council's face had lost a lot of its color. "But I asked for a volunteer. No one was forced."

So anyone could have used the Commanding Voice on him before departure, I thought, but instead of accusing anyone, I simply announced, "This will need a thorough investigation." Instinctively adding Queen's Magic to my voice, I commanded the gathered dragons, "Until further notice, no one will leave the settlement without permission from me, the Head of Council, or Telanuel."

The dragons gasped but bowed and murmured something that could be taken for agreement. Blood pulsed through my veins and roared in my ears. It felt good to be in charge. I turned to Telanuel. "You'll personally speak to every person and dragon who was involved with the travel arrangements. Use the truth chamber."

"Yes, Your Highness." Telanuel bowed, and a fist clenched around my heart. Had I really begun to order the dragons around as if I already was their queen? I watched the dragons file out of the throne room with drooping tails.

"I'm not sure if it was wise to use Queen's Magic on them," the Head of Council said.

As much as I agreed with her, I didn't explain or apologize. Right now I had bigger problems than the approval of dragon society. I had to find Nicole and then we had to organize a search for the lost princess. After all, the Chinese couldn't go without a royal family to rule them for long. Wordlessly I strode toward the exit.

"Your Majesty." Telanuel followed me. "I think it will be safer if I stayed by your side. The current events suggest that Mordekay has at least one ally. Who knows what will happen if you travel unprotected."

I nodded and remembered a few questions I'd been wondering about for a while. "Why is Mordekay still scheming? We turned him into a human. And why would a dragon, any dragon, follow a human? He's mad."

"Mad he might be," Telanuel said, "but he's got a vision where all the dragons in the world, united under one queen, will force humans to do what's best for them. The way they pollute nature, overpopulate their own cities, and generally make a mess of everything they touch, is a danger to every living creature on Earth, not just to us dragons. I'm not averse to his ideals either. I just do not agree with his methods."

Thoughtfully, I gazed at Telanuel. He knew more about Mordekay's motives that I'd ever cared to learn. Obviously he was a good Chief of Security.

"I'd be honored if you came along," I said. Feeling a lot safer with him at my side, I spread my wings and set out to find my friends.

Colin stared at the night sky, but no dragon silhouette appeared. Where was Lydia? Where was White Crow? He'd messaged both of them half an hour ago and had expected them to arrive within minutes. Harm led them higher and higher into the mountains, forcing them to climb steep declines every so often. Judging by the excited hopping of the little pebble they were following, they got closer to their target with every step. In regular intervals Harm confirmed the increased intensity of the scents on the trail. They urgently needed backup … now!

Colin's fingers trembled as he pulled himself over yet another ledge. What if he lost Nicole? Would it have been better never to know her? It would have saved them so much trouble, wouldn't it? But deep down in his heart he knew his reasoning was wrong. The fact that Mordekay was planning to use his sister for one of his evil schemes had nothing to do with his love for Lydia. The true question was, would he be strong enough to be a true partner for Lydia at all times? He pressed his lips together. How could he? He was nothing but a human.

A shadow passing over him made him look up. It was Lydia with a big, green dragon in tow. Finally! The backup. He glanced at the pebble, which was hopping up and down excitedly, barely waiting for Harm to scale the next rise. Like lightning, he realized that his heart thumped in a similar fashion when he just thought about Lydia. Now that he could see her beautiful dragon form land on a ledge not too far above them, warmth flooded his body and he felt strong enough to take on the world. Gone were all of his doubts. True, he would never be strong enough to protect her or to console her if something went wrong. But at the same time, he'd never, ever stop loving her. His heart filled with tears and determination in equal parts. He'd give his life for her if necessary. With renewed strength, he climbed on.

"We need to be very quiet," Harm whispered and looked back at him. "No calling out to Lydia or Mordekay might hear."

"I know." Colin smiled even though it didn't sit well with him that Harm thought the warning necessary. He'd never give away their only advantage.

They reached the ledge Lydia and the green dragon had landed on. Behind it was a patch of even ground in front of a gigantic vertical cliff. A small hole, just big enough for a grown-up human, led into a cave. The pebble hopped faster than ever and vanished through the hole. Harm held out a restraining hand, but Colin hadn't even thought about hurrying after it. The cave had to be Mordekay's hiding place and it would have been stupid to simply storm in. They lay down behind a meager bush clinging to the rocky soil. It wasn't much but provided at least a little bit of cover.

Colin looked around for Lydia. Where had she hidden? Was there a hint of white behind the big boulder on his right-hand side? He squinted when something big and dark and green suddenly blocked the stars.

The dragon swooped down on them and its tail slammed against Harm's temple. Colin's friend toppled unconsciously to the ground. Colin managed to roll out of the way, but when he got up to shelter behind the big boulder, he slipped. His head crashed against the rock and the world went black.

Nausea forced Harm to open his eyes. Pain pulsed through his head and he felt like vomiting. Instead, he kept his eyes closed and breathed deeply. The staleness of the air told him he was in a cave, and its fragrance suggested the presence of mashed herbs. Mordekay had always liked to use spells that required herb extracts, so it seemed reasonable to assume that he had been dragged into captivity. The iron bars digging into his back confirmed his suspicion. So the green dragon who had knocked him out must be Mordekay's ally. He blinked and looked around for the fiends.

It wasn't an easy task since the cage he was in was rather crowded. Beside Luke, Colin and himself, it held Lydia, still unconscious, White Crow, just opening his eyes and looking around in confusion, and Herbert in his human form, out cold too. Drat. There went their backup.

Also, Angie in her dragon shape was chained to the wall and … Harm's heart nearly missed a beat … Blackfeather's huge dragon head was lying on a golden table beside a stone slab that held Nicole.

A giant fist squeezed his heart until he struggled to breathe. Mordekay was nowhere to be seen, but Harm didn't doubt that he was up to something bad. The way Nicole was lying on the stone slab made him fear the worst. As he stared at her with burning eyes, a single thought echoed through his mind. *I love you, Nicole.*

A quick glance around showed him that the green dragon was preoccupied, looking at something at the back of the cave.

Mordekay was still not back, and a small, white Chinese dragon lay curled up in a corner. If he wanted to free Nicole, this was probably his only chance.

"Take care," he whispered to White Crow, who had turned and focused on the scene around them too, and to Luke, who held Colin on his lap gently slapping his cheeks. White Crow nodded, and Harm exploded into his dragon form.

It was the fastest transformation he'd ever done, and it shredded the cage, spilling its contents everywhere. With a single leap. Harm was at Nicole's side and grabbed her hand to pull her up. "Run," he said.

"Can't." Her gaze went over his shoulder. "Cover your ears. Queen's Magic."

Without questioning her, he slapped his clawed paws over his ears. The words aimed at him dampened and the urge to stop moving wasn't strong enough. At the last possible moment he dodged the green dragon's tail. The green dragon attacked him again. It was an unfair and uneven fight. With his hands over his ears to avoid the small Chinese dragon's commands, Harm didn't stand a chance. Also he was much smaller than the green dragon. After a couple of successful evasions, the tip of the green dragon's tail ripped through his flesh and slammed him into a wall. It was followed by the green one's head. Harm screamed with pain when several of his ribs broke. Still, he didn't stop fighting.

"I love you, Nicole!" He roared his pain and his confession through the cave again and again until his ears rang despite being covered. Surely no one could hear the Chinese dragon's Commanding Voice now. At the same time his hind legs clawed and kicked, keeping the green dragon at a distance.

From the corners of his eyes, he saw Luke run toward the green dragon, a jagged piece of the iron cage in his hand. He wanted to yell at him to stay away, but he had no air left for that. Behind the green dragon, the Chinese dragon stared at the fighting wide-eyed, trying to hide in a narrow niche. She was very clearly afraid and for a short moment, Harm felt sorry for her. A little to the side, White Crow and Herbert were just picking up metal pieces of the destroyed cage.

Luke slashed at the green dragon, evading its claws and tail with practiced ease. *Oh yeah, he's a knight.* Harm's legs buckled, and he sank down with the wall in his back for the moment. He needed to regain some strength, and then he'd carry Nicole out of danger.

Twentieth Chapter

When Harm tried to help her off the stone slab, Nicole realized she was able to move. Still, she remained. She couldn't simply flee and leave the fight to her friends. Mordekay was up to something bad, and she seemed the only one capable of stopping him. She lay back and observed the situation. The Chinese princess was trying to squeeze into a niche much too small for her. A few feet away from her, Lydia was lying on the ground, still unconscious. Mordekay stood at the cave's far end, unconcerned about the melee, crushing more herbs in a mortar.

When Harm's pained confession rang through the cave, Nicole's heart contracted. How could he be in love with her? He was a dragon. Dragons didn't fall for humans ... but then she remembered that Lydia was a dragon too. The painful screaming lasted, twisting Nicole's heart harder and harder. If only she could do something to stop Harm's pain. She longed to walk over to him. Maybe Lydia could teach her how to use her magic to heal him. Her gaze clung to his face. Despite the scales and the long horns on his neck-shield, he was the most beautiful of the few dragons she'd seen. She didn't dare to think of his human body. It distracted her too much.

"Mord!" The green dragon roared. "Get your sorry arse over here and help us."

"One more minute." Mordekay stepped up beside Nicole, and her head whipped around.

The dragon inside the Native American made her skin crawl. It was as if she could see the wrongness of the twisted features.

He held a knife dripping with greenish juices, and his voice held a note of Command. "It's time, my lovely. Now, don't move."

Nicole felt the ribbons take hold of her, just as Harm called out his love again. Anger surged through her, burning away the invisible threads as if they didn't exist. When the knife jerked down, she twisted. Instead of her heart, it cut deep into her shoulder. She screamed.

"Drat!" Mordekay twisted his knife and pulled it out. Blood flowed from the wound and he caught it in a clay bowl. Nicole sat up, reaching out to topple the bowl, but Mordekay was faster. He stepped aside until he stood right beside the golden table with the black dragon's head and pulled the knife through the palm of his host body's palm.

The wound in Nicole's arm kept pumping blood and she felt her strength ebb. There was nothing she could do, using her bodily strength to stop Mordekay. She would have to use her magic. But how? She hadn't had any training at all. She could kill everyone in the cave including Harm and Colin, the two most important people in her life. Could she risk that?

She didn't wait for herself to make up her mind and began to gather every bit of magic she could muster while watching Mordekay. He carefully counted seven drops of the blood from his palm into the bowl, pushed the lip of the dragon up and squeezed the bowl through a small gap where a sizable stone forced the jaws apart.

Nicole felt magic surge into her from the stone slab she was sitting on, just when the dragon swallowed the blood. The body of the Native American hosting Mordekay slumped. Nicole looked around to see who had knocked him out, but there was no one near. Could he have done it deliberately with his own spell?

"Hurry, Mord," the green dragon called.

Nicole felt as if she was bursting with magic. Hunger growled in her stomach like an angry wolf, but that didn't matter just now.

The black dragon blinked, lifted his head and roared. "Just a sec," he said with Mordekay's voice. He bent down and opened his mouth to swallow his former host body.

And Nicole released the magic. "Do what needs to be done," she whispered. Her body collapsed on the stone slab.

I drifted through the white fog knowing that there was something … something important that I should be doing. Like waking up. But a melodious voice had told me to sleep, and I found it hard to argue with it. For the longest time, I drifted without knowing who I was or where, but slowly, slowly, my mind returned. The white fog was familiar. Where had I encountered it last?

Something golden flashed through my returning memory. Of course! My parents. How could I forget about them? Where were they, and why was I cut off from the Queen's Magic and all of my ancestors? I tried to move deliberately, but that was harder than I had thought. Looking down, I realized that I was wrapped in black threads like the prey of a spider. Who had done that?

I looked around and there was nothing but the white fog. I closed my eyes and felt around.

There. A tendril of magic. Tender and very different from the magic I normally used. It tasted of stone, but it had gone through fire too, a long, long time ago. I called it to me, and it came, bringing with it a whole wave of magic.

The threads capturing me burnt and crumpled. I rode the wave of magic like a surfer and looked for my parents. As I burst into the brightness that was Queen's Magic, I hurled the wave at my parents, begging them to help. Not just me, but my friends too.

"We'll do whatever we can, but to become real enough to truly help, we'll need your reality." Mom nudged me gently with her snout and I slung both arms around her. "The magic Nicole gathered won't last for long."

"I'll stay here for as long as it takes." I let go of her just as something pierced my body. The pain was dulled by the distance between me and my body, but the agony was still sharp. Someone was tugging my body away from where it was before. "Hurry. Help us."

My parents absorbed Nicole's magic and popped out of existence in the realm of Queen's Magic, while I curled up and tried to cope with the pain.

A wave of tiredness swept through Nicole. She felt as if she'd been eaten alive and then spit out. Her arms were too weak to lift her torso up, so she stared at the human body beside the gold table with her cheek on the cold stone. The giant dragon mouth with the sharp teeth hung frozen over it, spittle dripping off teeth as long as her pinkie. *Please, Blackfeather, wake up,* she thought at the lifeless man, but he didn't move. Her eyes were so heavy. Nearly as heavy as her heart.

Unable to rise, she glanced around. The knight-girl, Colin and White Crow circled a green dragon. The Chinese dragon was still trying to hide, and Lydia was out cold on the floor. She tried to find Harm. One last glance was all she needed, but he was nowhere in sight. What had happened to him? Her pulse sped up. Despite her utter exhaustion, she tried to sit, but she fell back after lifting her face an inch.

"Mord, we're leaving," the green dragon shouted. His voice nearly burst Nicole's eardrums. She could see the others flinch. The dragon grabbed a big wooden crate and hurled it through the cave's exit. "Come on, Meiming, let's go." He hurled himself at the entrance, shifting at the last possible moment, and then he was gone. The Chinese dragon followed him in a blur without shifting. Her sinuous body allowed her to shoot through the opening like an arrow. Nicole noticed something dangling from her front paws, but couldn't make out what it was due to the small dragon's speed. Now only Mordekay remained, and he seemed frozen in place.

But then Nicole noticed that his teeth had crept closer to Blackfeather's still immobile form. Whatever her spell had done, it wasn't enough to save Harm's father.

Wake up! She willed him to rise. Instead, her eyelids drooped. She was so tired. If only she could close her eyes and sleep, but she couldn't. She tried to summon more magic, tried to pull some more from the stone to wake Blackfeather, but both her body and mind refused cooperation. Everything she saw, like her friends running after the green dragon, only registered on her brain in slow motion. She knew she'd overdone it. Badly. If only she could have saved Blackfeather, dying wouldn't be too bad. She blinked and looked around once more, hoping for a final glimpse of Harm. He had to be somewhere, hadn't he?

Then she felt someone's presence at her side. Warm arms helped her sit, but she was so weak, she couldn't turn. But it could only be one person. "I'm sorry, Harm. I tried to save him." Her voice was barely more than a sigh.

"You did very well." The voice was female, and strength flooded from her into Nicole's body. "Your magic helped Lydia to fight back."

Nicole turned her head and looked into the face of a woman so much like Lydia, it had to be her mother.

"Is this enough?" the former queen asked when Nicole sat on her own. Nicole nodded, dumbfounded. She'd been saved. Of course, her stomach still hurt from hunger, but the pain was bearable. She'd pull through. Lydia's mother smiled. "Then go and help the others."

She stood up, shifted into her dragon form, and joined a second dragon whose scales shone golden in the cave's strange light. Their roar broke Mordekay's freeze.

The black dragon took one look at the royal pair. To Nicole's big surprise, his facial scales paled to a dark gray as he hurled himself aside, just as the golden dragon's tail whipped toward him.

"But you're dead. I killed you myself!" Mordekay evaded the tail of the white dragon at the last possible moment. Without waiting for an answer, he fled, scraping his wings on the narrow entrance before he remembered to shift momentarily. The white and the golden dragon followed him, flying through the stone as if they weren't real. And naturally they couldn't be. Nicole smiled. *Hunted by his own nightmare,* she thought. *What a fitting punishment.* Then she turned away, determined to find Harm.

When Harm's consciousness returned, he found breathing hard. Then his gaze fell on his hand. It was clearly human. Had he really changed shape when he was unconscious? What did that say about him? He sighed and moaned with the pain. Every move of his chest caused spasms to run through his body. Still, he pushed the pain aside because the hand he had noticed wasn't his. It belonged to Nicole who crouched beside him with a worried frown on her face. He only had eyes for her. The worry on her face was the most beautiful sight ever, and if he'd die this instant, he'd be a happy man.

"Silly idiot," she said and crouched beside him. "Let me see." She prodded his ribs. Harm moaned, and she stated the obvious. "Broken. Don't you know that ribs can't take a bashing?"

Before he could answer she closed her eyes and bent forward. Her soft, warm lips pressed down on his snout. His eyes opened wide, and he forgot to breathe. But only for a second. Then a heatwave raced through him, and he turned into a human instantly.

His lips were on fire.

He closed his eyes too and allowed the tingling heat to fill all of his senses. Nicole's vanilla scent was so intense, the heat in his body became a boiling inferno. He longed for more—much more—than this kiss. Flames seemed to dance over his lips as her tongue entered his mouth. *Mother of all dragons, can the world get better than this?* The burning felt so real, so hot, that he worried it might burn Nicole. He just had to peek, but aside from Nicole's beautiful face there was no visible fire. He relaxed into the embrace, trying to ignore the spikes of pain whenever he breathed. His ribs would heal. Dragon bodies were good at that, and fast. Harm let the heat of his passion drive away the remnants of the pain, sucked in the enticing scent of his love, and was lost to the world.

Twenty-first Chapter

*B*lackfeather opened his eyes and stared at his hands in confusion. They were no longer pale. Not daring to hope, he touched his face. The hawkish nose was back, as were his smooth, stubble-free cheeks. It was his body, his very own body. A hickuppy sigh escaped his lips before he could get a grip on his emotions.

Fighting tears of relief, he looked around. A cave? How did he get here? Then he remembered the dragon council's envoy. What was his name again? Ah, yes, Telanuel. He'd convinced Angie that Lydia needed them, and they'd followed him into the mountains. After that, everything was dark. He looked around the cave he found himself in, when a familiar figure strode through the entrance. White Crow. His eyes narrowed. The man hadn't been too friendly when he'd been Mordekay's slave. On the other hand, you couldn't really blame him, considering what Mordekay had done to him. Blackfeather nodded to the man and tried to smile. It still didn't come naturally. Maybe it never would. White Crow nodded too and walked over to

Angie, who still hung from the wall. She seemed to be coming to her senses too.

"They got away." Two youngsters entered the cave. One he recognized as Colin, the other seemed to be a girl, although it held a makeshift weapon like a pro. They were followed by one of the few friends Blackfeather had ever had.

Herbert was in his human form, small, hump-backed, and old. "We need to regroup."

Blackfeather stood up to walk toward the group, but first he looked around the cave some more. His gaze fell on his son, lost in the kiss of a red-headed girl. His next smile was far more successful.

Angie woke from the most beautiful dream she'd ever had since her husband had died. She'd seen his face as clearly as if he'd been standing right beside her, and she just didn't want that dream to end. So she wasn't one bit surprised to see White Crow's face when she finally opened her eyes. But when he spoke—real words reaching her ears—the shock set in.

"I'm so sorry," The sun-tanned fingers of White Crow's hands caressed her cheeks. "I longed to contact you, but I just couldn't."

She closed his mouth with a kiss; a kiss she'd longed for for much longer than she'd cared to think about. A flood of pictures flowed from his mind to hers. Lydia, the death of her parents, the draconian world, even a distant view of her house, and every single picture was accompanied by sorrow and pain. And she understood.

Colin's head whipped to and fro as he searched the cave, and his hands grew cold. "They took Lydia!"

His words echoed through the cave and every face turned toward him. Even Harm and Nicole stopped kissing.

"They what?" White Crow's eyes were wide with panic.

"I only saw Telanuel take a crate along," Herbert said.

"That's the amplifier I built." Luke stared at the ground, his makeshift sword hanging down. "Punish me."

"Why would we do that?" Herbert took the sword from her hand and patted her shoulder. "You've been helping us fine when bad came to worst."

"But I deserve it." Luke still didn't look up. Colin could feel her pain, but it was nothing compared to the emptiness in his chest. Where had his heart gone? He forced himself to listen to Luke's explanation. "My father was Europe's last knight, and he always wanted a successor. So I was quite the disappointment until I managed to convince him that I could be a knight too. I never questioned his view that dragons are personified evil."

"To err because you love someone doesn't deserve punishment." Herbert hugged the girl, and tears started to flow over her face.

"But I trusted Mordekay. I thought he would…" Her eyes widened. "Oh God, he'll enslave all humans with my gadget. Especially since he managed to convince my aunt to give him my computer program that goes with it."

Colin's stomach twisted. Mordekay … and Mordekay again. Everything was his fault. If anything happened to Lydia, he'd kill the guy. And even if not, it'd be better to eliminate him.

"All that's very interesting, but what about Lydia?" White Crow looked as if he'd seen a ghost. Are you sure they took her?"

"I saw the Chinese dragon carry something when she fled." Nicole stared at Colin just as wide-eyed as White Crow. "Could that have been her?"

"Lydia can access Queen's Magic. She'll break free and return to us. I'm sure of that." Angie tried to calm them all down, but it didn't work for Colin.

He picked up Luke's makeshift sword and turned toward the exit. "I'll find her, and then whatever god they believe in help the kidnappers." He walked out of the cave without looking back to see if his friends were following.

A single thought dominated him. Life without Lydia wasn't worth living, so he might as well die trying to get her back.

to be continued

A Reminder: What Happened Before

*L*ydia loses her parents and her memories in a car accident and has to live with a foster mother. When she starts school again, she meets Harm, a young dragon who can turn into a dragon. A little later she encounters Colin, a human she immediately finds likable.

Lydia discovers that she's meant to be the next dragon queen which she rejects vehemently. There reason for that is that the other dragons won't accept the love she feels for Colin.

Mordekay, a black dragon, encourages Harm, his son, to woo Lydia. He hope she'll bind with him (dragons love and bind only once). But he's not counting on hope alone. With the help of his slave Blackfeather he kidnaps Lydia, Harm, Colin and Nicole (Colin's sister, a big fan of Fantasy books), to perform a ritual that'll put him into Harm's body.

After that he wants to force Lydia magically to bind with him. But Lydia's heart belongs to Colin already, which ruins Mordekay's plan. Therefore he orders Nicole who is under his spell to pour Dragon Bane over Lydia. Dragon Bane is deadly for dragons, even in small doses. Colin manages to foil this plot and gets doused in the liquid which thankfully only results in a strong sunburn for him.

At the same time Blackfeather prevents Mordekay from taking over Harm's body. Instead he ends up in Mordekay's. Now Mordekay is trapped in Blackfeather's body.

Harm discovers that Blackfeather is his real father and not Mordekay. Together they carry off the unconscious Mordekay while Colin, Lydia, and Nicole drive home.

JUMA'S RAIN
Romance-Fantasy set in Stone Age Africa

„An enjoyable fantasy with a complex heroine…" Kirkus Review

The sun's rays parch Juma as she leads her all male family toward the main village. Nothing and no one will stop her from becoming the chieftess' apprentice. So she ignores the heat. Everything will be better near the lake. But the fields that should sprout green by now lie bare, with precious soil cracked and dry. Even the lake, thought to be everlasting, dwindles.

Juma discovers that heat dæmon Mubuntu is out of control and that the rain goddess is still sleeping. But only Netinu, the chieftess' son, believes her, and he seems more interested in courting her than in the welfare of the tribe.

With her dreams going up in flames, Juma prepares to battle the dæmon and wake the goddess—and maybe, in the process, prove herself worthy of becoming chieftess.

ISBN 978-3-95681-011-4
auch als eBook erhältlich

AMADI, THE PHOENIX, THE SPHINX AND THE DJINN
A tale from the Arabian Nights in three parts

Amadi enjoys the busy frenzy the souk and tries to escape the harem her stepmother rules as often as possible. Unlike her sister Bülbül she feels caged, not protected. When Bülbül becomes engaged against her will, Amadi longs to evade a similar kismet.

Luckily a master thief wants her as an apprentice, and she grabs the chance to live like a boy. Too bad that she and her teacher become targets of a jackal-headed god of death and an assassin when they accept an assignment from a magic-using customer.

Who wants them dead so badly remains a mystery she must solve to survive. And now that she fell head over heels in love, she very much wants to live. With her life spinning out of control, will her skills be enough to save her ... and, maybe, the caliphate too?

ISBN 978-3-95681-065-7
auch als eBook erhältlich

THE DWARF AND THE TWINS
SNOW WHITE AND ROSE RED
Treasures Retold 1

Once upon a time in a world where magic and technology collide with unexpected consequences…

When Martin helps a pregnant woman to flee from the king's men, he doesn't know that the twins she bears will change his solitary life forever.

What if the Brother's Grimm misunderstood the dwarf in the original tale of "Snow White and Rose Red"?

The book includes a bonus story and the original fairy tale.

ISBN 978-3-95681-028-2
auch als eBook erhältlich

Leave your eMail address so I can inform you about new releases, and this book will arrive as an eBook in your Inbox shortly after

http://www.katharinagerlach.com/readers

ROYAL SWANS
THE SEVEN SWANS
Treasures Retold 7

Once upon a time in a world where magic and technology collide with unexpected consequences...

When neighboring royals visit the kingdom, Prince Laurent declines the princess' advances with dire consequences. Turned into swans, he and his brothers flee, followed by their sister in a flying machine. But then, they crash-land on a cemetery. Can they regain their humanity before the enraged princess catches up with them? And what about the strange ghost Laurent feels drawn to?

What if Hans Christian Andersen overlooked "The Seven Swans" part in breaking the curse?

The book includes a bonus story and the original fairy tale.

ISBN 978-3-95681-074-9
also available as eBook

www.ingramcontent.com/pod-product-compliance
Lightning Source LLC
Chambersburg PA
CBHW051436170626
46809CB00006B/2491